Full Moon over the
Ghost City Of Jerome Arizona

Are Ghosts Real?

The Story of "Belgian Jennie"

The Richest Madam in the Arizona Territory

By Peggy Hicks

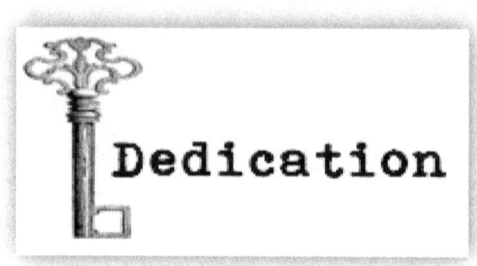

Dedication

To my mother,
Dorothy Louise Hicks

My mother taught me that the
ability to achieve something
starts with a desire,
but it is the
practice, practice, practice
that makes it possible
to obtain your goal.

*Available on Kindle
and Amazon.*

*Sold in gifts shops in
Jerome, Arizona 86331*

Author's Notes

Are ghosts real? This age-old question seems to have plagued most of humanity for centuries and the evidence that ghosts do exist is sometimes compelling. In the following first two chapters of this book, I will attempt to shed some light on this phenomenon. Another question commonly asked is, "Have you ever seen a ghost?" I usually answer, "I think so."

As for this account of Jennie Bauters, aka Belgian Jennie I have tried to maintain the most accurate narrative possible given the available facts about her. The characters and circumstances within this story are based on real people and events. I have also incorporated authentic dialogue and documents when available. However, in light of the scarcity of records from that time period, I have utilized a few dramatizations to further the story and fill in some of the missing pieces.

Introduction

Jennie Bauters was from Antwerp, Belgium. She sailed across the Atlantic destined for America in 1896. While in the U.S., Ms. Bauters opened several houses of ill repute and her story details some of the hardships and violence one might expect from a true Wild West tale. Belgian Jennie, as she was later known, eventually became the richest madam in the Arizona Territory. They called these women soiled doves, prostitutes or Madams. The truth is they were whores. They knew it and everybody else knew it.

She kept a leather journal that cataloged all the dirty little sexual secrets of many of her clients. The key to this locked book always hung on a silver chain, securely around Jennies' neck.

Her story is filled not only with financial success, but also with brutality. This brutality also affected many of her girls, her customers and eventually even Jennie herself. In fact, Belgian Jennie was viciously murdered one morning by her lover "CC" as she ran barefoot down a dusty road, dressed in her night clothes.

Her burial was controversial because some folks did not want her buried in the same graveyard as their beloved family members.

In 2010, one-hundred and five years later, Jennie's grave was accidentally unearthed and desecrated by construction workers. As if they were trash, her bones were thrown into a Home Depot bucket and are now stored in a county yard facility in Lake Havasu City, Arizona.

Since these disturbing events, there have been reports of an apparition resembling Belgian Jennie, haunting the darkened streets of GoldRoad, Oatman, Jerome and Kingman Arizona. The woman is always seen dressed in night clothes and is carrying a human skull. Some have attempted to approach this mysterious woman, but when pursued, she simply disappears into the darkness. Could she be scouting out her old haunts of GoldRoad, Oatman, Kingman and Jerome looking for her lover, Clement C Leigh to return his skull? Some believe that this is indeed the ghost of Belgian Jennie stuck between this dimension and the next.

After reviewing the evidence presented in this book, you can decide for yourself if you believe ghosts are real.

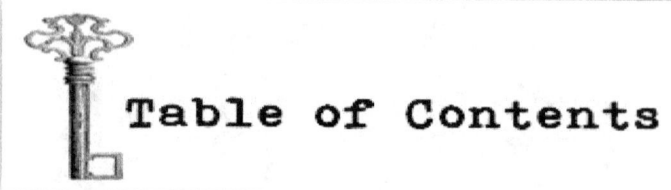

Table of Contents

Are Ghosts Real?

So, are ghosts real? People have been asking themselves this question for thousands of years. Most consider them to be the souls of the dead.

The simple word "ghost" creates images of translucent, flowing spirits in all forms, shapes and sizes. They are usually imagined as disembodied spirits and are often seen as vague or fleeting forms; thus, the white sheet routine.

In today's world, interest in the paranormal is on the rise and growing more popular by the day. As the interest in ghosts, spirits and the paranormal increases, we see a corresponding increase in books, movies and TV shows revolving around ghost hunting and the paranormal. The Old English words for ghost is "gast" which means soul, spirit or breathe of life. Ghosts are feared all over the world and have been since humans began to examine dimensions outside of the present one. But despite widespread sightings and stories dating back a millennium, we still have no definitive proof that ghosts actually exist.

Skeptics say that any so-called paranormal evidence has a rational explanation and that those who believe in ghosts are only fooling themselves. Believers, on the other hand, say that the skeptics are blind to the evidence that's right in front of them.

The common belief is that a ghost is the soul or spirit of a deceased being. Believers feel that these spirits manifest themselves in many different ways. They appear in different places and often to different people.

Here are a few:

Orbs: These are probably the most photographed type of anomaly. They can be solid in nature, partially transparent or translucent balls of light seen hovering about. It is true that the vast majority of orb-like images that appear in photographs do have a rational explanation. They usually turn out to be dust, water, reflections or insects. Some, however, are convinced that they are basically ghosts moving around in a state that requires the least amount of energy to manifest.

Apparition: These will take on the shape and form of a person and usually appear to be almost transparent. Apparitions are usually immediately identified as ghosts.

Photographic: This refers to the type of ghost that only shows up in a photograph or even a video. Usually, the person taking the photo or the subjects in the photograph will state that they never observed anything unusual there at the time. However, when the photographs are later viewed, random faces or images appear.

Cold Spots: These are commonly experienced in places where paranormal activity has been reported. The cold spot never has a natural cause and is usually contained in a small localized area, sometimes 10 degrees colder than the surrounding area.

Poltergeist: Poltergeist comes from the German words "Noisy Spirits". These spirits are said to interact by screaming, throwing objects or slamming doors. They can be mischievous or even aggressive and usually appear and disappear from areas without warning.

Keep in mind that ghosts are said to be earthbound spirits. Using this scenario, a ghost would be a spirit who hasn't gone into the light (the light of the spirit world). So if you believe in haunted houses in the traditional sense, it would be earthbound ghosts who are haunting them. Ghosts are defined as deceased humans, while demons and angels are extraterrestrial and not of earthly origin.

Extraterrestrial: If you believe that God and his angels are from heaven, then that would make them extraterrestrial. If Satan and 1/3 of the angels rebelled against God's Kingdom as in (Revelation 12), then Satan and 1/3 of the angels that became demons are also extraterrestrial.

Extraterrestrial Angels: Angels have always been known as messengers or servants of God. Most religions will argue that angels have power over spirits and because of this status; they never experience a material or physical life. Sometimes in their service to God, angels assist humans by guiding them and even intervening at times with "miracles". Sometimes a living relative or loved one may appear to us when they are in trouble. We may even learn of a loved one's pending demise when that person seems to appear before them, possibly to say a last goodbye.

Of course, since that person is still alive, they couldn't possibly be a ghost. This may simply be the message of an angel. Also, people who have had a near-death experience have reported seeing their loved ones on the "other side", but then returned, because it was not their time to go.

Extraterrestrial Demonic Entities: These demonic spirits should be avoided at all cost. It is widely accepted that these energies were never human. They are also sometimes referred to as "Demons". They thrive on negative emotions like fear, anger or depression and can wreak havoc on an entire household. They can be attached to objects, buildings, a person or even an entire family. The reason for their presence is usually due to some dark practice which has called them forth. Demons are entities that never had a mortal human form and are extraterrestrial.

Again, the most popular theory in the American culture is that ghosts are the spirits of humans who have died but have not yet "crossed over" to heaven or hell. They are not angels or demons. It has been suggested that the soul may "sleep" or enter a "holding place" until Judgment Day.

There are nearly as many theories as to what a ghost is, as there are paranormal investigators.

Science tells us that nothing in nature, not even the smallest atomic particle can disappear without a trace. Think about it. Who is right, who is wrong and where is the proof?

Is the Bible the final authority on this matter? Many Christians will say that they have seen a ghost or felt a presence, but they have a hard time fitting those experiences in with their Christianity. Because of this, it's not unusual for Christians to feel torn about this subject.

What does the Bible say about ghosts? In the King James Version of the Bible, the word *ghost* occurs 108 times. The *Holy Ghost* is mentioned 80 times and *"familiar spirits"* are mentioned 28 times. An example of the word ghost is when Jesus appeared to the Disciples in *Luke 24:35*; Two men from "Emmaus" told their story of how Jesus had appeared to them as they were walking along the road and how they had recognized him as he was breaking the bread. Luke *24: 36.* Just as they were telling about it, Jesus himself was suddenly standing there among them. "Peace be with you," Jesus said. *Luke 24:37;* the whole group was startled and frightened, thinking they were seeing a *ghost. Luke-24: 38, 39.* "Why are you frightened?" Jesus asked. "Why are your hearts filled with doubt? Look at my feet. You can see that it's really me. Touch me and make sure that I am not a *ghost* because *ghosts* don't have bodies, as you see that I do." *Luke 24:40*; "as he spoke, he showed them his hands and feet that had been nailed to the cross."

Before the Europeans brought Christianity to the Native Americans, they had their own beliefs about death and the afterlife. Most Native American tribes took death and burial rituals very seriously. One common belief that still influences death rituals is the focus on helping the deceased be comfortable in the afterlife. Rituals included placing food, weapons, jewelry, tools or pots within the burial site for use by the deceased in the spirit world. They believed that any disruption in the cycle would cause unrest for the spirits, who in turn, cause unrest for the living.

Many tribes of the Navajo Nations in the Southwest and Four Corners region referred to ghosts as *"chindi"*. It was believed that if someone did not get the burial rites that were due upon death, their spirit was doomed to remain on the earth. Also, disturbing or desecrating a grave or a burial ground could cause spirits to become active and no longer at peace. In turn, the ghost or spirit would torture the living, afflicting them with what they called, "ghost sickness".

Symptoms of ghost sickness included nausea, fever, fatigue, hallucinations, the sense of being suffocated and other worrisome symptoms, like unexplained misfortune.

The Indians believed the best way to avoid ghost sickness was to first perform proper burial rituals. These included obliterating footsteps from around a grave and disposing of the dead person's belongings appropriately. After that, everyone would stay well away from the burial grounds. They believed that there could be lingering ghosts who never had a chance to vent their anger on people and could still do so. Of course, many of these symptoms could be attributed to other causes, but the belief is strong that it's a sign of a ghost attempting to take one of the living with them.

These beliefs still linger among many tribe members to this day. Some archeologists and authorities still hire Native American religious figures to perform protective rituals when tribal burial grounds are disturbed. The common belief is, if a person dies peacefully and of natural causes, they do not become a ghost. In a natural death, the spiritual body slowly disentangles itself from the physical body. As the dying process starts, the person loses their desire for food or water. Internal organs start to fail moving upward toward the crown. Their hearing and thoughts are the last to go. This is the time to tell them how much you love them.

Then the person experiences intermittent loss of consciousness until the loss becomes permanent. At this point of death, whatever pain or agony the person is suffering ceases and a total sense of peace and tranquility descend onto them. He or she usually registers this transition with a calm and peaceful look on their face instead of the agonizing grimace they may have had. The body is now limp. At this point, their spirit becomes astral (*separated from the physical body.*) From here on, no healer in the world can resuscitate the departed person.

Much research has been done to determine why someone might become a ghost. The popular presumption is that a haunting seems to occur mostly under the following circumstances; when death is sudden and traumatic, the lack of a proper burial, desecration of a grave or tombstone or some other type of vandalism. In some cases, the spirit may leave and then return to the place where their death occurred. Some spirits may even take out revenge on the wrongdoers. Additionally, some believers assess that if the person was bad-tempered in life, they will have the same bad temper as a ghost. If they were pleasant in life, then they will continue to be a pleasant ghost.

Other reasons one might become a ghost include;

Murder–Occasionally, in unsolved murders, a ghost will not "move on" until the murder is solved.

Accidents –A haunting following sudden accidental deaths such as car wrecks, drowning, falls or fires is far more prevalent than in natural deaths.

Suicide - The torment that a suicide victim felt will often cause them to remain here in ghostly form.

Broken hearts - A family member may selfishly not want to let go of their deceased loved one and cause their spirit to remain earthbound.

Greed - Sometimes humans are unable to let go of their earthly possessions. This is also believed to cause haunting.

Lack of a proper burial - If the spirit believes he or she did not receive what they believe is a proper burial, they may remain as ghosts.

Desecration of a grave – Even though these spirits have already passed on, they will often return if vandalism or other desecrations of the grave occurs.

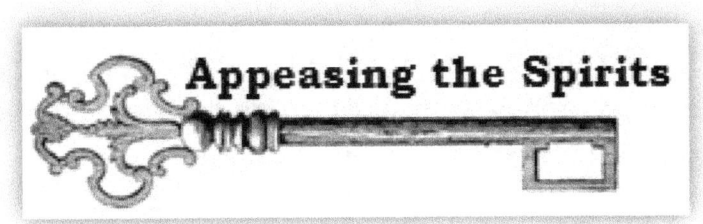

Appeasing the Spirits

Many early burial customs were actually practiced to protect the living and not the dead. They were done to appease the spirits who were thought to have caused the person's death. Such ghost protection rituals and superstitions have varied extensively depending on time and place, as well as with religious beliefs. Many of the following examples are still in use today.

1. It was customary to stop the clock at the exact time of death. The doors were unlocked and windows in the room were opened to ensure the spirit could escape.

2. Placing coins on the eyes of the deceased was to pay the "Fairy Master" who would, in turn, assure their loved ones would make it to heaven.

3. Covering the face of the deceased with a sheet comes from pagan beliefs that the spirit of the deceased escaped through the mouth.

4. Another, was to carry the deceased out of the house feet first and entering the cemetery the same way. This would prevent the spirit from looking back and beckoning another member of the family to follow.

5.   The tolling of the bells was actually not to announce a death or pay homage to the deceased, but a means of scaring away evil spirits.

6.   The use of tombstones may go back to the belief that ghosts could be weighed down. The deeper the grave and the heavier the headstone, the less chance a ghost could escape.

7.   Some people even considered it necessary for the funeral procession to return from the graveside by a different route than the one taken in with the deceased. This way, the departed's spirit wouldn't be able to follow them home.

8.   Some of the rituals we practice at funerals today may, in fact, be rooted in the simple fear of spirits. Beating on the grave, the firing of guns and cannons, funeral bells, and wailing chants were all used by some cultures to ward off spirits and scare away other ghosts at the cemetery.

9.   Native American tribes often burned or destroyed the home of the deceased to keep their spirit from returning.

10. Women of ill-repute were often ostracized by society. Some private and religious cemeteries would not allow prostitutes to be buried among the blessed and moral and could not be given a Christian burial.

Many times, public cemeteries would agree to take them, only to be placed in a pauper's grave or even buried outside the cemetery's perimeter. These graves were frequently unmarked and soon forgotten. Belgian Jennie was one of these women. After her brutal murder in 1905, her body was laid to rest just outside the cemetery's boundaries in Kingman Arizona.

Since the beginning of time, humanity has come up with numerous ways of dealing with the dearly departed. The manner in which Americans view death, as well as the manner in which the dead were buried, has adapted over the years.

During the days of the Puritans, (16th century) very little fanfare accompanied the burial of the dead. Death was viewed as fire and brimstone, a punishment from an angry God or the act of the feared grim reaper snatching away their loved ones. Skull and crossbones were commonly placed on grave markers.

The Civil War era also brought about changes in the way the dead were dealt with. Since the men were busy in battle, the responsibility of mourning fell mostly to the women who chose a more honorable type observance to the fallen. Grave markers were replaced with symbols of angels and clasped hands in honor of their husbands and sons who lost their lives in war.

Queen Victoria became the role model for proper mourning etiquette with a more tender and loving service for the deceased. People began to sing religious songs, writing epitaphs and eulogies, more in line with today's customs.

Today, chances are you will die at one of four places; at the scene of an accident, on the way to the ER, in a hospital or at home under hospice care. Sadly, the odds that the last sound you will hear is, "I love you" are quite low. Most people die with the noise of hospital equipment ringing in their ears, the crunching metal of a car wreck, or the sound of screaming sirens. If you die on the scene of an accident or in the ambulance, your spirit will pass from you on some busy highway, floating over the roofs of McDonalds and Jiffy Lubes. If you survive the trip to the hospital you will be strapped to a gurney and wheeled into the ER. Medicine or surgery may prolong your life. However, sooner or later we will all face that last day.

Hospice care is another option. This option allows terminally ill people to die naturally in the familiar surroundings of their own home. When death occurs, the County Coroner will be called.

Once we know we are dying, we can cooperate with our doctors to select specific actions that will bring death as gently as possible. These are the four legal ways, with the doctor's approval, we can end our lives.

1. Increasing pain-medication.
2. Withdrawing life-supports.
3. Terminal sedation.
4. Voluntary dehydration.

If you die in a hospital your IVs will be removed and you'll be stuffed into a black plastic body bag. Some kid working his way through college will then wheel you down the hallway to the morgue. On the way, he will wink at the young nurse he wants to date and probably wonder what's for lunch. Your lifeless body will be placed on a stainless steel tray and slammed into a cooler. Despite the cold, your body quickly begins to decay.

If you are not cremated, a mortician will pump your blood out and replace it with a sweet-smelling fluid, glue your eyelids shut, force your swollen tongue back into your mouth and wire it closed. They'll apply their cosmetic products to make you look as if you are still alive and just sleeping. The funeral directors will press their scripted pitch to those still in shock while arranging for overpriced payments for your funeral. You'll be placed in a casket and the most expensive pillow you have ever owned will be placed under your head. Eventually, you'll be moved to an elegantly adorned "home" built on the profits from the dead. With a specific purpose, the undertakers will speak in a tone and cadence that will set the mood for mourning. Your next of kin, weeping, will sit on expensively covered sofas and chairs.

The air will be filled with depressing music as people pay their last respects before you are eventually placed into a grave.

If you are cremated, your corpse is placed in a combustible container and placed in a furnace. During incineration, the body is exposed to extreme heat fueled by natural gas, oils, or propane. The flames burn the skin and hair, contract and char the muscles, vaporize the soft tissue, and calcify the bones so that they eventually crumble. Your small bones, like fingers and toes, are all consumed in the fire. After your remains cool, a manual inspection of the mixture using strong magnets and/or forceps is made to remove foreign objects i.e. dental work, surgical screws, prosthesis, implants, etc. Your larger bones are then run through another process that pulverizes them into the consistency of pasty white beach sand. On an average, it takes about one to three hours to cremate a human body, thereby reducing it to 3-7 pounds of ash-like remains.

If you do not have an urn, your ashes are placed in a box and given to a relative or representative. Your ashes might be entombed in a mausoleum, placed on a mantel, stored in a closet, dumped into a garden or maybe even scattered on the Las Vegas strip. This may all sound quite heartless and even gruesome to some, but one thing we can all agree on, is that we will not live forever and for most of us, the subject of death is an uncomfortable one.

The Ship Manifest

Belgian Jennie's Story

A ship manifest indicates that Jennie Bauters was born in Schaerbeek, Belgium in 1862. Jennie Bauters or "Belgian Jennie" as she would later be known was thirty-four years old.

Her son, Joseph Phillipe Bauters was fourteen when they left Antwerp, Belgium and embarked the steamship, "Obdam" in Bologna, France. From there they sailed to Rotterdam, Holland, then across the Atlantic destined for Ellis Island in the United State of America. Jennie spoke Dutch, English and Walloon, a sister language to French. She was well-educated and had money. Now separated from her abusive husband, she and her only son dreamed of a better life in America.

There were three types of accommodations on the Obdam ship that brought immigrants to America. There was first class, second class and third class or "steerage" as it was called. A third class steerage ticket was about $25.

The cabin-passenger list showed that Jennie Bauters and her son Joseph Phillipe Bauters had second class tickets aboard the S.S. Obdam. One second class ticket to cross the Atlantic in 1896 cost about $143, which was a tidy sum back then. The consumer price index estimates that $143.00 in the year 1896 would be about $5,000.00 in the year 2016.

The U.S. immigration law went into effect in 1893. Every prospective ship's passenger had to answer up to 30 questions before acquiring their ticket. This information was then recorded on the ship's manifest. Questions included, among others; name, age, sex, marital status, occupation, nationality, ability to read or write, race, physical and mental health, last residence and the name and address of the nearest relative or friend in the immigrant's country of origin. They were also asked whether they had ever been in prison or in an institution. A medical inspection was also imposed on all passengers traveling to America during the great wave of immigration at the turn of the 20th century. Once emigrants arrived at the port of departure, a few obstacles remained. Emigrants had to pass various physical exams to ensure a certain level of health before embarking. This was to prevent the spread of disease while on board as well as to prevent diseases from being carried to the destination country.

Passengers were inspected for possible contagious diseases such as Cholera, Plague, Smallpox, Typhoid, Yellow Fever, Scarlet Fever, Measles, and Diphtheria. The disease which resulted in the most exclusion was Trachoma, a highly contagious eye infection that could cause blindness and even death. At that time, the disease was common in Southern and Eastern Europe, but almost unknown in the U.S.

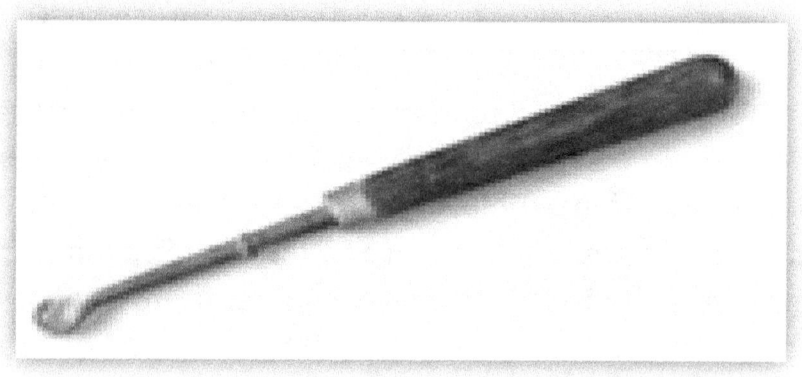

Button-hook

The "button-hook men", as they were called, were the most dreaded of all officials. These were doctors who checked for Trachoma by turning the eyelids inside out with their fingers, a hairpin or a button-hook to look for inflammation on the inner eyelid. Needless to say, this was an extremely painful experience.

First and second class passengers were not required to undergo the inspection process. Instead, these passengers underwent a brief inspection aboard ship; the theory being that if a person could afford to purchase a first or second class ticket, they were less likely to become a liability in America due to medical or legal reasons. The Federal government felt that these more affluent passengers would not end up in institutions, hospitals or become a burden to the state.

Crossing the Atlantic could take anywhere from two weeks to a month based on the ship and the weather. Third class or "steerage" passenger space was usually very limited and was located deep in the bowels of the ship. These passengers were led down narrow gangways and steep metal stairways. The noise became intense and oil fumes thickened as they squeezed past the ship's machinery into the dark and dismal lower decks. This was the worst part of the ship and subject to the most violent motion. They were now in steerage and this was to be their prison for their entire month-long ocean journey. Although most people adjusted to the constant rocking and bouncing of the ship, others spent the entire trip nearly bedridden with nausea. Some lie in their berths for most of the voyage in a seasick stupor and any kind of food eaten often ended up on the floor.

Only saltwater was available for toilets and bathing and they were completely inadequate. The odors of unclean bodies, the stench of nearby toilets, unattended vomit and inadequate ventilation made for some horrible foul smelling air. But in spite of these miserable conditions, the emigrants had faith in the future. On calm days, passengers would play cards, sing, dance and talk to pass the time.

There were probably as many reasons for coming to America as there were people who came. It was a highly individual decision. Historians agree that four social forces were the chief motivators for the mass migration to America at the turn of the Twentieth Century. These included religious persecution, political oppression, economic hardship or simply a dream of fortune.

(When a person leaves his country to take up permanent residence in another country, he or she becomes an emigrant as well as an immigrant. A person is an emigrant upon leaving their homeland and an immigrant upon arriving at their destination.)

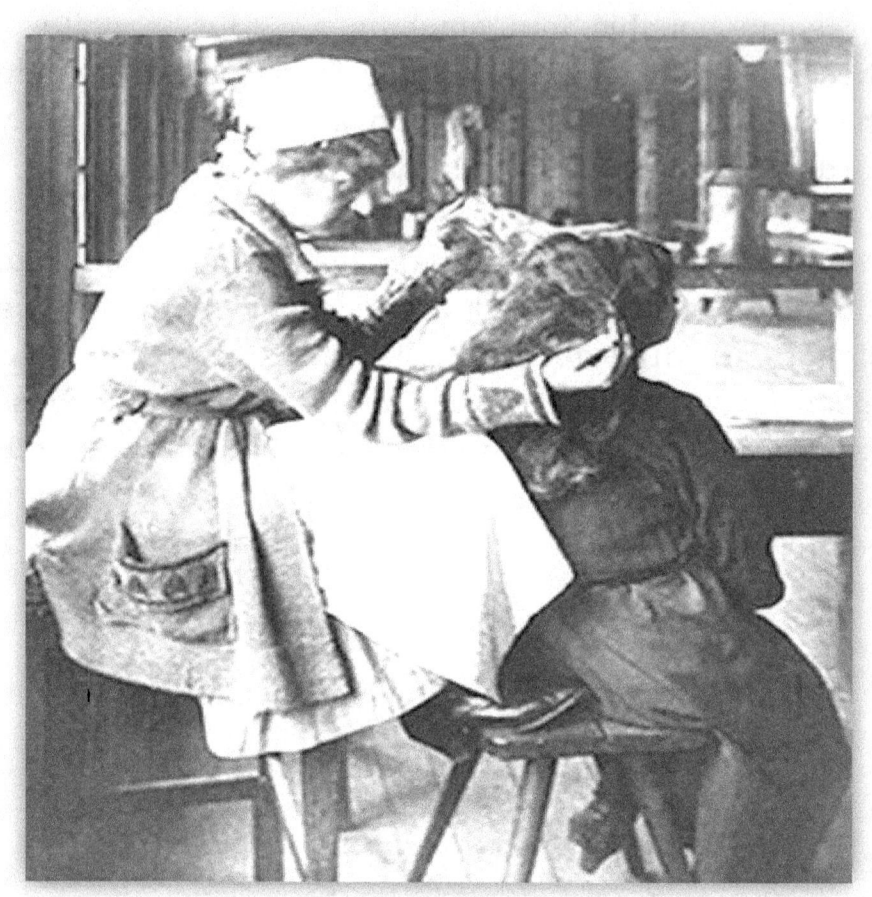

Jennie Bauters' luxurious wavy brown hair was examined for lice and both her and her son's belongings were fumigated. After all the questions were answered and medical exams and vaccinations were completed, they were led to their onboard accommodations. Still stinging from the shots and disinfectant, they rested in their berths as the ship set sail to the United States of America.

After a grueling, month-long sea voyage, the colossal green copper patina of Lady Liberty came into view. Just beyond the statue, about a half-mile to the Northwest was their destination, Ellis Island.

On July 6, 1896, Jennie and her son, Joseph arrived at Ellis Island, New York, USA. Excited, yet uncertain of the future, they stood on the dock and thanked God their feet were back on solid ground. The air was finally fresh and clean. It had been the toughest ordeal either of them had ever endured. Their lengthy journey, however, was not over.

Jennie had made arrangements for their luggage to be processed and loaded on a westbound train. With train tickets and a box lunch in hand, they boarded the train to the Midwest. Their ultimate destination was Chicago, Illinois with its substantial French/Canadian population.

Jennie always had an unstoppable, entrepreneurial spirit that was admired by many. She came to America to seek a better future and prayed that there would be better opportunities for both her and her son.

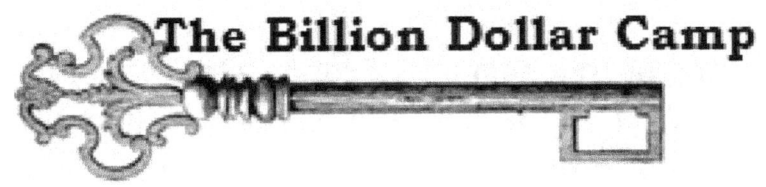

The Billion Dollar Camp

Shortly after her arrival into the United States, Jennie left her son Joseph with the nuns at St. Ignatius School in Chicago. Jennie then boarded another train, this time bound for the woman starved, copper mining town of Jerome, Arizona.

Jerome, Arizona began as a small copper mining camp consisting of nothing more than a few tents and some crudely built shacks. The town of Jerome quickly evolved and throughout its mining history yielded over a billion dollars worth of copper, gold and silver. This enormous production eventually gave the town its nickname, "The Billion Dollar Copper Camp".

Jerome was founded in 1876 and established a post office in 1883. Jerome, Arizona, once known as "The Wickedest Town in the West" was named after a New York City banker and philanthropist named Eugene Murray Jerome. His cousin was Jenny Jerome, the mother of the former Prime Minister of the United Kingdom, Winston Churchill. Although Eugene Jerome was a major investor in the town's copper mining operation, he never made a single visit to his namesake town.

The town of Jerome, unique in its location, clung precariously on a thirty-degree mountain slope over

5000 feet above sea level. It sat high above the Verde Valley with the red rocks of Sedona clearly visible in the distance. In 1888, Montana Senator William Clark bought the United Verde Copper Company and proceeded to put Jerome on the map.

Clark was a cunning entrepreneur who didn't want to depend on mules and wagons to haul his precious minerals, so in 1895 he built a narrow-gauge railroad just for the job.

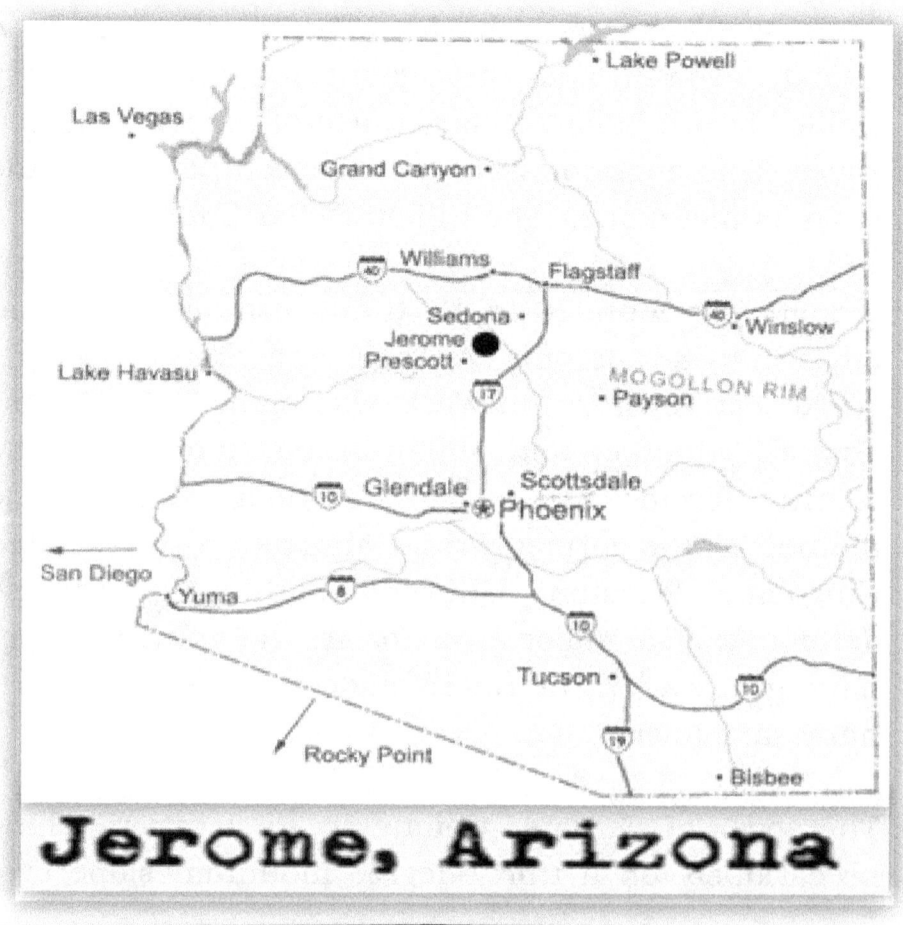

Jerome, Arizona

The United Verde & Pacific Railway originated from Jerome Junction near Chino Valley. The line had 86 curves on the short 26 miles of narrow gauge track and became known as the crookedest line in the world. It ran six days a week and brought people in from all over the globe to work in Jerome's copper mines. Prior to the turn of the century, Jerome's population was primarily composed of men representing over forty different nationalities.

The United Verde & Pacific
Jerome Az. Circa 1899

There were Mexicans, Chinese, Irish, Italians, Hungarians, Polish, Slovakians, and Germans. Most wives stayed behind to take care of families, while their men ventured out to strike it rich. Along with the miners came businessmen, saloonkeepers, gamblers, hustlers and of course, no mining town would be complete without its share of soiled doves.

The social history of Jerome parallels the social history of nearly all of the early mining camps in Arizona. Like all of them, Jerome had a good-sized population of men working in the mines and living in its boarding houses. The majority of the population was comprised of 90% young, single men compared to the town's 10% women. Jerome sometimes became a violent place and had a reputation for gambling, alcohol, drug abuse, gunfights and other mayhem. Needless to say, Jerome was not the type of town most would choose to raise a family.

Many of the first women to arrive in Jerome consisted of those of low moral standards. A few of their names appear in arrest records or health licenses for prostitution, but most of their identities are nowhere to be found.

During Jerome's glory days, the miner's worked shifts around the clock. When the men were not working the miles of underground tunnels beneath the town, they were raising hell in the many bars and bordellos above it. Gambling became epidemic. In fact, it was said that most men carried a deck of cards in their pocket and a revolver in their boot.

No. 43 Jan 15, 1899

City Physician's Certificate of Examination.

This is to certify that I have carefully examined
MISS KATIE GULLAHORN and find her in a sound and
healthy condition, and not infected with any contagious
or infectious diseases.

This Certificate expires March 25, 1899.

Fee paid, $2.00.   C. E. SMITH, M. D.,

C. E. Smith

City Jerome, Ariz.
Health Physician

Early in Jerome's history, houses of prostitution flourished in the very heart of the business district. They were generally taken for granted and some felt that prostitution actually performed a necessary function. At one point, it was estimated that more than 100 prostitutes practiced their trade in Jerome. The town boasted of 13 hotels, a large number of saloons and at least eight houses of prostitution.

As mentioned, Jerome was at times a rough and rowdy place. The copper mines ran twenty-four hours a day with three shifts. The sidewalks, saloons and restaurants were constantly crowded with men buying food, gambling, drinking and on occasion, fighting. In Jerome's early years, the town had no sewer system or public trash removal and residents tended to throw their refuse out the back door or into the street. This stench, plus the toxic sulfur fumes from the smelter operation wreaked havoc on everyone's lungs.

The sweet smell of French perfumes and the pretty petticoats of the fairer sex were in stark contrast to the hard-rock miner's daily grind. This afforded a lucrative opportunity for any woman willing to rent her body. Many prostitutes who rose to the top of the industry and became successful madams, owned more wealth than other women in the United States. The madams sometimes referred to as "landladies" were usually former prostitutes. A few of these "ladies of the night" who possessed the necessary business sense, eventually graduated into owning and managing their own brothels. Now they could then take care of the business portion of the brothel and let their girls do the entertaining. A very special customer might be entertained by a madam, but generally, she did not sell sexual favors.

Three of the more renowned madams were Nora Butter Brown, who was the first madam in the new copper camp; Jennie Bauters, aka Belgian Jennie. Belgian Jennie later became the richest madam in the Arizona territory. Then during the roaring twenties came The Cuban Queen from New Orleans.

Some of the lesser known women operated from the less elegant area known as the "Cribs". Visiting the cribs was a definite step below the nicer bordellos with their upscale amnesties, but it was definitely safer than doing business with the common streetwalkers. It was like the old adage; "You get what you pay for".

Encounter of Two Legends

Nora "Butter" Brown once told a tale about a chance encounter of two Wild West legends at her Jerome saloon in 1879. It was November 27th on the Saturday night after Thanksgiving. Nora's brothel/saloon had only been open a few days. Her liquor order had just arrived and everybody in town was there to celebrate. One of the fellows in the bar was a young scrawny cowboy about 18 or 19 years old. He was covered in dust from days on the trail.

He said his name was Henry and he had just delivered a small herd of cattle from the New Mexico Territory to a buyer near Phoenix. He heard a rumor that there was a new "house of pleasure" up at the Jerome camp and just had to check it out for himself.

His Colt 44 pistol hung low on his right side, in a worn leather holster tied to his thigh. You just had the feeling that he could make that gun jump into his hand in a heartbeat. All the locals at the saloon were captivated by Henry's charismatic personality and tall tales. The newly hired saloon gals sidled up to him and were hypnotized by his charm. There was just something about him that made the local boys want to stay on his good side.

.

Later on that night, a second outsider rode up and tied his horse to the hitching post. He looked to be a whole different type of man than Henry. This man was tall, thin and fit, and was put together more like a city fellow. He wore a flat-brimmed hat and a vest with a gold watch chain stretched from pocket to pocket. His gun was covered by his broad cloth coat. He looked over the swinging saloon doors with caution before entering. His foot steps seemed silent as he walked across the planked wooden floor of Nora's saloon and quietly took a seat at a table across the room. His back was to the wall.

Because of the way he was dressed, Madam Nora immediately thought he might have some money to spend on a lady, so she took a bottle of rye whiskey, a couple glasses and leisurely walked over and introduced herself.

Nora wasn't a very pretty woman and she would often say, "Boys, I know I'm not much to look at, but wait till you see my girls. You're gonna love me then". And it was in fact true that she had some very pretty saloon gals. The tall outsider didn't seem much interested in a romantic interlude, so they talked a little business.

Henry, the young cowboy shook off one of the saloon gals and walked over to the table. With a big smile on his face, like he wanted to sell you something, he said, "Is this a private party or can a friendly stranger join in?"

Nora watched as the tall outsider sized up the young cowboy and his gun. "Have a seat cowboy. I'll buy you a drink."

Henry pulled up a chair backwards, sat down and took a drink right out of the bottle. He said, "Looks like you maybe oughta be deal'n Faro in some fancy saloon in Dodge or Abilene. You look a little too high falutin for this establishment. Maybe you took a wrong turn somewhere huh?"

The tall stranger replied, "Just passin through son. I'm headed for my brother's place over in Prescott. I'm helping him and his family move to Tombstone".

"My name's Henry McCarty," said the young cowboy as he reached across the table. The tall outsider shook the cowboy's hand and said, "Wyatt, Wyatt Earp". The young cowboy smiled from ear to ear as he looked around the room. "I was think'n that was you. I saw you in Dodge City once." Standing up, he put his hands on his pistols and announced, "Wonder who's faster with his guns, me or Mr. Wyatt Earp?" Wyatt calmly and slowly took a small drink of whiskey and quietly said, "You don't have to do this son". At this point, both men acted like two coiled-up rattlesnakes ready to strike. Wyatt instinctively stood and stepped in front of Nora as if to shield her. At that very second, someone ran into the bar yelling, "Apaches are stealing all the horses down at the stables!" Several patrons bolted for the exit; just as two war-painted Indians came crashing through the saloon doors, demanding bottles of whiskey. One Indian pulled Henry outside and in broken English said, "Let's go. We got a fresh one for you."

Henry jumped on a horse, still smiling like it was a church social. He yelled back at Wyatt, "Maybe some other day, Mr. Earp. Once I get paid for these nags, maybe I'll look you up in Tombstone. How'd that be?" "By the way, my friends call me Billy."

Wyatt answered, "It would be my pleasure son."

Henry and the war-painted Indians rode off with several stolen horses while firing their pistols in the air.

Nora later admitted that she was scared that night and actually wet herself. She had heard stories of the Apaches and what they do to white women. Well, that whole incident seemed to rattle Wyatt's nerves a little so Nora and Wyatt ended up adjourning to her chambers upstairs where it was a little quieter.

Nora later said in an interview, "Now don't go ask'n for no rude details. A lady doesn't talk of such things, but I will say, Mr. Earp stayed the whole night. Now that I think back on it. If it hadn't been for that little rascal Henry, I might not of had the opportunity to bed a legend such as the likes of Wyatt Earp".

Nora found out later that Henry, the young cowboy was the now legendary Billy the Kid. Turns out he was in cahoots with the local Yavapai Indians and they weren't Apaches after all. Henry set the whole thing up just to keep the locals distracted while he stole the horses.

During this time, Prescott was the Capital of the Arizona Territory. Wyatt's older brother, Virgil Earp was living in Prescott and had just been appointed US Marshall of the new boomtown, Tombstone. Wyatt was on his way to help Virgil move.

Before Wyatt left Jerome, he bought a team of horses and a buckboard wagon. He planned to convert the wagon into a stagecoach and start a transportation line in Tombstone. When he arrived in Tombstone, however, Wyatt found two established stage lines already running, so instead,

he got a job working for Wells Fargo and Company. Wyatt was hired to ride shotgun and responsible for

the safety of the cargo. The shipments frequently contained silver bullion and were prime targets for the "Highwaymen". Whether because of his reputation, or pure luck, no shipment guarded by Wyatt Earp was ever attacked. Several months later, in October 1880, Wyatt was appointed Deputy Sheriff of Tombstone and quit his job with Wells Fargo. Within two years,

Tombstone went from a population of 100 to 6,000, making it Arizona's largest town between New Orleans and San Francisco. In 1881 the Earp brothers, Wyatt and Morgan, along with their friend, Doc Holliday were deputized. They were key participants in the "Gunfight at the O.K. Corral". Even though the gunfight only lasted about 20 seconds, Hollywood film makers turned the scuffle into a full length Hollywood classic movie.

Billy the Kid also became a legend, rustling cattle and horses and raising hell all across the country. The same year of the gunfight at the OK Corral, Billy the Kid was killed in Fort Summer New Mexico by Sheriff Pat Garret.

William Wingfield was only 19 years old in 1879. He helped put the roof on Nora's brothel and claimed to have been in Nora's saloon that Saturday night on November 27, 1879 when Billy the Kid made off with Jerome's local livestock. He witnessed the encounter when Wyatt Earp and Billy the Kid came close to a shootout over drinks in Nora Butter's bar in Jerome.
Later, in 1903, William Wingfield interviewed Nora at her home in San Diego, California and documented this story. William Wingfield wrote a piece printed by Hartcort Press in 1946 entitled *Jerome, the Wickedest City*. Nora's account also appeared in *True West Magazine*. It is believed to be the only time these two Wild West legends, Wyatt Earp and Billy the Kid ever

met. William Wingfield later became a successful rancher here in the Verde Valley.

He lived to be ninety-two years old and died in his sleep at home in 1951. He swore until his dying day that this story is true.

Nora sold her bordello to Jeanie Bauters, aka "Belgian Jennie" in 1896 and retired in San Diego, California.

In 1905, Nora (Butter) Brown was shot to death by her opium-addicted husband. Ironically, Jennie suffered the same fate in the same year. She too was shot to death by her opium-addicted boyfriend, Clement Leigh in Goldroad, Arizona.

The fact that Jennie purchased a brothel so soon after her arrival suggests that she had substantial funds. It is not known for sure, but given her age, Jennie may have had previous experience as a madam in Belgium before coming to the United States.

Jennie renamed her business, The "Honky-Tonk House of Light Love" and went on to become a very successful madam in Jerome. She was later said to be the richest madam in the Arizona Territory.

Honky-Tonk House of Light Love

Jennie Bauters aka "Belgian Jennie"
Is the woman standing in the middle
on the upper balcony wearing the
dark dress. Circa 1898

In the early spring of 1897, the Verde Valley echoed with the sound of one long whistle as the United Verde and Pacific train arrived in Jerome. This time, aboard the narrow gauge, was a woman from Belgium named Jennie Bauters. She would later become known as "Belgian Jennie".

On November 27, 1897, approximately a year after she bought the brothel from Nora Brown, Jennie registered in detail, her real and personal property with the Yavapai County Recorder's office. She claimed each item as "sole and separate". She stated, "I am a married woman, but I earned all my possessions by my own labor or by trading, while living separate and apart from my husband." She made it perfectly clear that her husband had not given her any money or aided her in any way in obtaining her assets. Jennie's filing with the Yavapai County provided a fascinating glimpse of her business sense. It reveals her as quite the perceptive businesswoman and property owner. Among other things, she owned bar fixtures, household furniture, musical instruments, an expensive lapel watch and other fine jewelry. Her personal home was built on three lots; twenty, twenty-one and twenty-two in Block Eleven on Boarding School Road. "The Honky-Tonk House of Light Love" was built on three lots; lot four, five and part of six in Block One. Three days later, she made out a *Will and Testament* naming her son in Chicago, Joseph Phillipe Bauters, her sole heir.

Jennie's usual attire exemplified the latest fashion trends of London and Paris and became a symbol of her wealth and social status. On any particular day, an example might be; a shirtwaist blouse with a tall collar, a long tailored skirt and a wide belt that accented a tiny, corseted waistline. Jennie had money and she usually dressed the part. Jennie's luxurious wavy brown hair was stacked softly on her head, in a style called a Pompadour.

*(**Pompadour** refers to a hairstyle which is named for Madame De Pompadour (1721–1764), mistress of King Louis XV. The style was revived as part of the Gibson Girl look in the 1890s. The men's version was worn by early rock and roll stars such as Elvis Presley in the 1950's.)*

On Christmas Eve in 1897, less than a month after registering her property and placing insurance on it, a terrible fire broke out. The reporter for "The Mining News" reported:

A man and his mistress were in a quarrel at "Japanese Charlie's" lodging house when a kerosene lamp was thrown. The lamp hit a wall and within minutes the building was engulfed in flames. From there, the fire shifted toward the East, consuming the "Peerless Saloon", another restaurant and then a barber-shop. Blocked by the Connor Hotel's brick walls, the flames turned to the North and destroyed another row of saloons including Jennie's brothel, "The Honky-Tonk House of Light Love".

Jennie could only watch from afar as the raging fire consumed her building that night. Jennie lost everything, including her personal jewelry and clothing worth an estimated $4,000. It was reported that her insurance on the structure paid $900.00 of the $1,500.00 in reported damages.

In spite of Jennie's loss, she was relieved that her girls got out and no one was harmed in the blaze. Jennie was determined to keep her business open and managed with tents for shelters until a new brothel could be constructed. Incredibly, within the next two years, Jennie endured two more devastating fires.

Most of these buildings were made primarily of dry lumber, canvas and other flammable materials. Fed up with her losses, Jennie decided to rebuild, but this time the building would be made of brick, stone and concrete.

Jennie took out a series of secured mortgages on her properties to rebuild her new brothel on Main Street. Confident she would no longer be plagued by fire, she spared no expense on its furnishings. Unfortunately, this new building made of brick, stone and concrete caught fire as well. Before the fire got completely out of hand and with her quick thinking, Jennie ran into the street and told the town's firemen that she would give them all free passes to her brothel if they would save her building. The firemen rose to the occasion and Jennie held true to her promise. They extinguished the fires of the burning building and in return, her girls put out the burning desires of the fireman for years to come. Jennie's story of "fire insurance" is still told to this day.

"Jennie's Place" was the three-story structures located on lots four and five and part of six at 136 Main Street in Jerome. "Nellie Bly's", the famous kaleidoscope and art glass store occupies this building today.

Nellie Bly is recognized as the largest brick & mortar kaleidoscope store in the world. The store has anything your geometric dreams could imagine. A historical marker funded by the Jerome Historical Society is mounted on the front of the building.

JENNIE'S PLACE

THIS BUILDING WAS ORIGINALLY A BROTHEL KNOWN AS JENNIE'S PLACE. IT WAS BUILT IN 1898 BY LEGENDARY MADAM BELGIAN JENNIE BAUTERS, WHO CAME TO JEROME FROM BELGIUM IN 1896.

THIS WAS HER THIRD BUILDING ON THIS SITE. THE FIRST BURNED DOWN IN 1897. HER SECOND BUILDING, PICTURED AT THE LEFT, WAS DESTROYED IN THE FIRE OF 1898.

JENNIE IS THE WOMAN IN THE BLACK DRESS IN THE CENTER OF THE BALCONY. THE CURRENT BUILDING, WHICH FEATURED THE FIRST CONCRETE SIDEWALK IN JEROME, IS ONE OF THE FEW IN THE BUSINESS DISTRICT THAT SURVIVED THE FIRE OF 1899.

WHEN JENNIE BAUTERS WAS MURDERED IN 1905, SHE WAS REPUTED TO BE THE WEALTHIEST WOMAN IN THE ARIZONA TERRITORY. AFTER HER DEATH, HER SON SOLD THE BUILDING TO JOHN M. SULLIVAN WHO CONVERTED THE BORDELLO INTO THE SULLIVAN HOTEL.

FUNDED BY THE JEROME HISTORICAL SOCIETY PLAQUE PROJECT

Jennie was a shrewd businesswoman and had many responsibilities as a madam. To attract women to work for her in this highly competitive market, she offered a higher wage than they would find in any other employment. She also provided free doctor visits, legal assistance, housing and meals. Jennie received 50% of all revenue taken in by her girls. She served overpriced whiskey to her clients and charged $2.00 per visit, which was just about a day's wage for a miner.

Often, madams like Jennie controlled their own health standards. If a man checked into the United Verde Hospital with a venereal disease, Jennie checked her records to make sure he hadn't been to her place.

It was well known that Jennie Bauters had a leather journal that was said to have cataloged the dirty little sexual secrets of many of her clients. She kept the key to the lock on a silver chain around her neck. It was in her best interest to keep her visitors' names a secret. After all, her customers might range from a lonely miner or rancher to a banker or even a sheriff. Consequences could be disastrous if word got out.

The town of Jerome was incorporated in 1899. Soon after, a newly elected city council enacted an ordinance forbidding anyone from advertising, passing out tokens, business cards or any kind of signage calling attention to any house of prostitution. Marketing for any individual women that worked in a brothel was also prohibited. Anyone violating the ordinance was guilty of a misdemeanor and subject to a five-dollar fine, plus court costs. Few people paid attention to the ordinances though, and business continued as usual.

The city also banned houses of prostitution from operating on Main Street. To get around that obstacle, Jennie simply opened her back door on Hull Ave and made that door the main entrance. This area would soon be known as "Husband's Alley". Jennie was an astute, 19th-century businesswoman and never missed an opportunity to promote her business despite any city ordinance.

Belgian Jennie is pictured in the following photo taken in 1897. She is the woman standing in the middle wearing a dark dress, wide belt and a lapel watch.

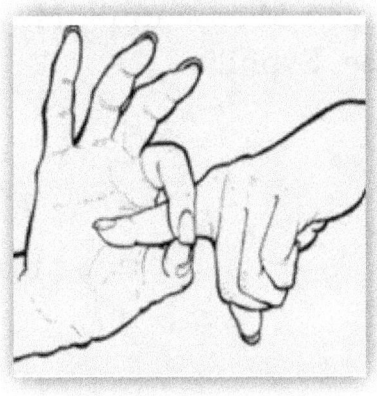

More telling is her hand jester with a closed fist, leaving a hole for her thumb to be inserted. Both of these hand jesters were a well-known advertising signal for sex among the prostitutes.

Jennie constantly had her share of troubles. She was always in and out of court. On February 8, 1898, she filed a criminal complaint against Gabriel Lopez, claiming he had stolen sheets, underwear, towels, her silver hairbrush, shirt buttons, gold necktie pins and the list went on.

On January 9, 1900, Jennie appeared with several of her girls as witnesses in a robbery involving three Mexican railroad workers.

The following month, Jennie testified at the inquest of one of her girls named Rose Ames who had died of an opium (laudanum) overdose.

In July of 1902, a man named Cartholdi Sequera shot another patron in the leg while the victim was standing in the hallway at Jennie's Place.

One of Jennie's working girls named Maggie Shultz died of a gunshot wound inflicted by Francisco Paco, a rejected suitor.

Another girl named Miss Fannie May contracted the infectious disease, Syphilis.

A Day with Fannie May

They called them soiled doves, called them prostitutes, called them women of ill repute or called them madams. The truth is, they were whores. They knew it and everybody else knew it. People sometimes smirk at the whole prostitute business, looking at these women as morally corrupt. For the most part, the majority of these women entered this type of work out of sheer desperation and poverty. Prostitution was in fact, a very perilous business.

Women in this profession suffered constant illness, financial difficulties and sometimes even violent abuse. Yes, it is true that these women laughed, drank, smoked, used drugs and raised hell more than most women, but they were also lonely, they feared for their lives and some even prayed and repented in their darkest hours. For most of them, it was far from a glamorous life and it's important not to automatically let the dark side of their profession overshadow the fact that they were also human beings. It is sometimes quite fascinating to take a look at who some of these women really were.

Fannie May was twenty-six years old and one of eight girls working on "the line" at Jennie's Place. The male clients waited in a lavish room on the ground floor. A slim maid in a spangled, short skirt and revealing top brought the men overpriced drinks while they waited for their turn with the girls upstairs. This practice loosened up both the men's nerves, as well as their wallets.

In a dark hallway on the upper floor, a small wood plaque hung over the door that said, "Fannie May."In the rear of the long hallway was an exterior door that led to a narrow outside staircase furnished with stout hand-rails. These stairs led to a privy (outside toilet) on the ground level. This staircase was only for egress and was used by any departing guest that wished to avoid meeting someone entering the front.

Inside the room, Fannie May handed an exhausted client (or "John" as they were called) his hat as she ushered him out the door. "Come back and see me anytime," she said with a fake smile as she quickly closed the door behind him. The word was, the waiting room downstairs was full of clients and the girls needed to pick up the pace. Fannie flipped over her sheet for the third time and it was still early in the evening. It was the miner's payday and she was expecting a busy night. It would not be unusual if she had fifteen to twenty visitors tonight.

The scarcity of women created a ready market for prostitutes. Although a woman could do quite well selling her services to the lonely miners, there was also a downside. The profession was usually plagued with violence, addictions and disease. Some in the business were even killed by their own clients, while others wasted away with drugs and alcohol. Pregnancy was also a major concern.

With a bar of soap and a wash pan, she washed up starting with her face, then armpits and then her crotch. She dabbed herself with perfume and sprayed some rose water around the room. She was well aware that the last thing a man wanted to smell was another "John" as he walked into the room.

Then, as expected, there was a knock on the door followed by the maid's announcement. "Fannie, you have a gentleman caller. His name is Hardy".

This was her fourth customer today. She opened the door. "Good to see you again," she said with a smile. Of course, no one used their real name in this business, not even her. Hardy's real name was Henry Townsmen. His wife, Eleanor Townsmen was the secretary for Jerome's water company and an acquaintance of Fannie's. Eleanor was unaware that her husband, Henry visited Jennie's Place at least once a week. Fannie took Hardy's money and slipped it through the narrow slot in the locked drawer of her dresser. Fifty percent was hers and the other half would go to Madam Jennie. Jennie kept good books and always knew what was going on in her place. At the end of each day, all her girls had to turn in their receipts, cash and all bar tokens if they wanted to get paid.

Henry, or Hardy as she called him, licked his finger, pulled off his wedding ring and placed it in his pocket. It wasn't the first time a man had removed his wedding ring at Jennies' Place. Her place did, after all, face the area known to all the locals as "Husband's Alley". Hardy sat on the edge of the bed with his pants down around the top of his boots. Seldom would a man take off his boots. That's why she always kept a rug or oilcloth at the foot of the bed. This kept the dirty boots from soiling her sheets.

Fannie approached Hardy with a wet washcloth soaked in a solution of iodine. This was an attempt to keep down venereal diseases. "At least married men bathed more often than unmarried men," she thought to herself as she washed Hardy. He reeked of alcohol. It was obvious he was on one of his binges and not in a very good mood. "Tell me I'm a very handsome feller," Hardy demanded.

"Indeed, you are a handsome man," Fannie responded. Suddenly, Hardy grabbed Fannie by her hair and shoved her face in his lap. "Not me, you damned whore!" He pointed at his crouch. "Tell him he's a handsome feller!" Fannie had been in the business long enough to know that most men that came to Jennie's seemed to think that they were gifted with something extra special. She had seen hundreds, maybe thousands of these and they were pretty much all the same to her. In the back of her mind, she wondered if he treated his wife, Eleanor this way. For the next several minutes she played with it and pretended to enjoy it. His rancid breath from liquor and cigars almost choked her as he kissed and licked at her face. Then, with his weighty body on top of her petite, one-hundred-pound frame, he grunted, groaned and dripped with sweat. All she could think about was how glad she would be when this was over. All she said was "Come on handsome, give me all you got."

Fannie worried about that little sore on her leg and prayed it wasn't Syphilis. In the beginning, she wore dark stockings to cover the curious sores. As it turned out, Fannie May was, in fact, infected with the highly contagious disease, Syphilis. She was unaware of how awful the infection really was until it was too late. It devoured her leg and sadly, Fannie later died of this horrifying disease.

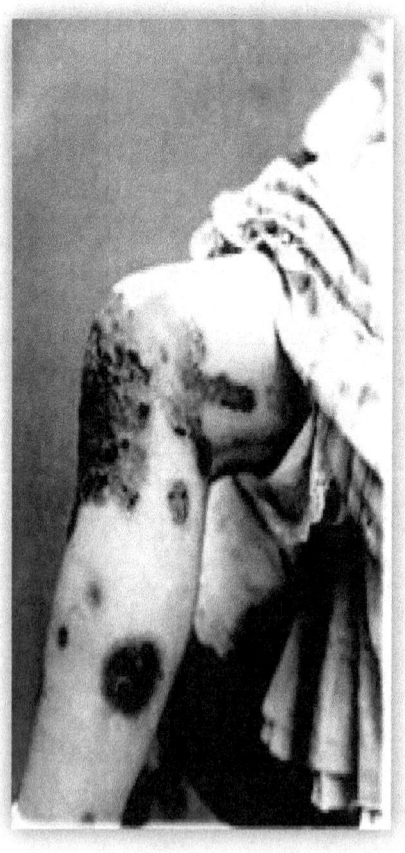
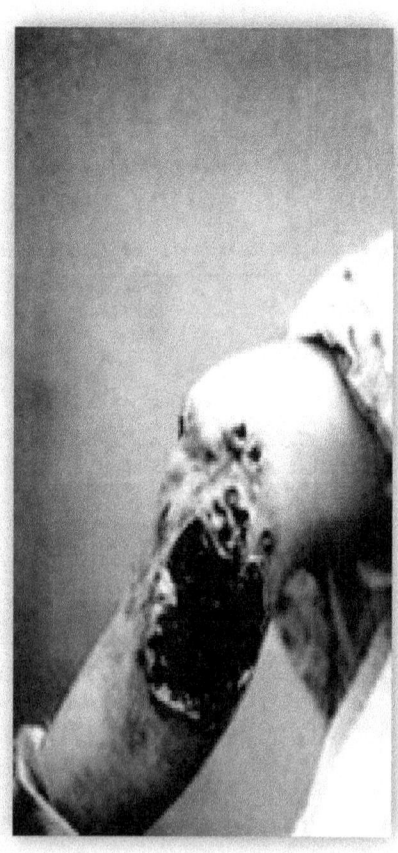

The woman in the light dress is believed to be Fannie May Ewing. This photograph was taken in the red light district on Hull Avenue. Some have speculated that she may have been intoxicated, given that she is leaning on a wall and appears to have been held steady by the girl in back.

If you went back to the 1800's you would find laudanum, also called 'tincture of opium being sold over the counter and without a prescription. Many women, particularly prostitutes used laudanum, primarily as a sedative and painkiller. It was prescribed for childbirth, menstruation, menopause, headaches, and other aches and pains. It was highly addictive and often used as an aid to commit suicide.

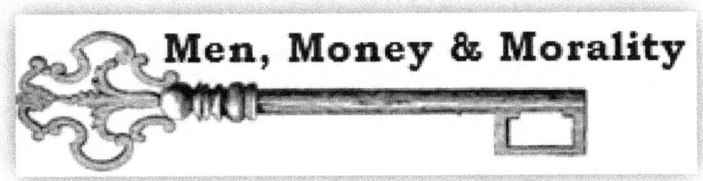

Now called OJ's Mother Load
(Copper Country Fudge)
Ice-cream, homemade candy and fudge

Winchester Bar, 337 Main Jerome, AZ.
Circa 1800's

Belgian Jennie operated her business in the mining camp of Jerome, Arizona for seven years. To stay on the good side of the community, she always gave money to charity and churches. Because of these contributions, the police often looked past many of the things that went on behind her closed doors. In this atmosphere, contemporary newspapers celebrated Belgian Jennie as a concerned and compassionate friend to the lonely miners. Jennie held the door open for the ugly, the misfits and the many men that had been injured in mining accidents. She gave the middle-aged and older men their last fling as they desperately tried to hang on to their youth. Often, fathers would bring their young sons to her for their first time, knowing she wouldn't trounce on their son's adolescent egos. Even a few wives of the miners were secretly appreciative of Jennie's services, although they would never admit it to her face. For some wives, sex was just too exhausting, too dirty or too inconvenient. Jennie also knew that not one of these ladies or gentlemen would even acknowledge her presence outside the seductive walls of her bordello.

In 1902, the clerk of the Yavapai county board of supervisors launched an investigation on Jennie's Place. The audit revealed that Jennie had been underpaying her business license taxes. City officials were profiting from all the fines and license fees that were being extracted from the "red-light district".

It seemed ironic that the very deputy sheriff collecting the fees was a regular customer of Jennie's. The ever-changing city ordinances and excessive fees were making it more and more difficult for Jennie to stay in business.

Jennie looked down from her second story balcony at the men gathered on the dirty street below. She took a long drag on her cigarette and bitterly whispered, "Money, Men, Morality. What hypocrites. These people are nothing but a bunch of damn hypocrites." In protest, she coughed-up some snot and spit it over the rail onto the street below.

The city was demanding more money and the avowed "churchgoers" were demanding morality. But that didn't change the nature of the business. In fact, she and her girls could barely keep up with the demand.

It was late morning in the summer of 1903 when Jennie woke to the sound of girls singing. It was Jennie's birthday. She was appreciative of the cake and the efforts her girls made to cheer her up, but the truth was, she was turning forty today.

Looking in the mirror, she saw the lines and cracks that circled her mouth and the crow's feet that surrounded her eyes. She called them "scratches of doom". She brushed her hair with her silver brush and noticed how the persistent gray in her temples was getting harder and harder to camouflage.

Yes, parts of her life had been fun, but it was now obvious that the years of hustling and reckless living had taken its toll. She sucked in her tummy, but keeping it in was impossible. It was obvious her thighs and backside were much heavier than they use to be. She knew her days in this business were numbered. She was no longer the attractive young woman that arrived at Ellis Island a few short years ago.

Jennie was secretly glad her friend Clement C. Leigh or "CC" as Jennie called him wasn't there for her

birthday celebration. He was ten years her junior and she didn't want him reminded of her age.

Jennie, like anybody else, longed for genuine human comfort and companionship. She knew in her heart that she was CC's enabler, but she didn't care. The attention he gave her made her feel young. Unfortunately the man she cared for seemed to be on a slippery slope between morality and immorality.

Clement C Leigh had just been arrested for breaking and entering and was sitting in jail. She always had a big soft spot in her heart for him. Like a moth to a flame, she would be there that afternoon, bail him out and pay his fine just as she had done numerous times before. Usually, because of his hot temper, CC always seemed to be in some sort of trouble. He was a handsome, persuasive and a charismatic character.

He was a Faro card dealer, a gambler and often abused both opium and alcohol. Court records show that he was arrested on several occasions while intoxicated and had threatened the lives of several of Jerome's reputable citizens with a gun. In the past, Jennie had always come to CC's aid and this time was no different.

The Jerome Marshal, Fred Hawkins considered Clement C. Leigh a troublemaker and a dangerous man. With reservations, Fred Hawkins released Clement C. Leigh into Jennie's custody. He ordered Leigh out of town and threatened that if Leigh ever set foot in Jerome again, he would lock him up and throw away the key.

Fred Hawkins was a tall slender man. He had reddish hair and a sandy mustache that drooped a bit on either side of his mouth. He had a long career, first as Deputy Marshal of Jerome from 1900 to 1904, then as Marshal until 1916. During that time, he had more than a few opportunities to find himself in conflict with Jerome's red light population. People that knew him said, Fred Hawkins would disarm a man if he could, wound him if that's what it took to subdue him and only kill if he must.

Clement C. Leigh knew that Fred Hawkins, the deputy marshal, was dead serious this time. He knew he had only one choice and that was to get out of town while the getting was still good.

Jennie had always been the one in control and since C.C. was released in her custody anyway, her resolution was to leave Jerome together. They would look for another town where the law wasn't constantly breathing down their necks. It was also important for Jennie to locate another boom town with a high male-to-female ratio in which she could continue her business. She heard of a brand new mining camp in Mohave County. It was about 20 miles from Kingman, Arizona. A prospector named Jerrez had discovered gold a few miles west of Oatman. The rich ore body gave rise to a camp called "Acme" and fortune seekers were swarming into the area.

Jennie and Clement Leigh hopped on the United Verde & Pacific train to Jerome Junction near Chino Valley. From there they boarded another train to Kingman Arizona. The last leg of their journey would be an all day, hot and bumpy wagon ride to check out this new boom town called Acme Camp.

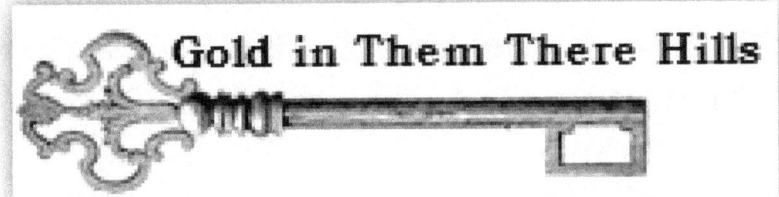

Gold in Them There Hills

It was estimated that more than two million dollars in gold ore was taken from the Gold Road mine in Acme camp, Arizona during its short duration from 1903 to 1907

In 1902 a post office was established under the name of Acme, Arizona to serve the three hundred people living there. In 1906 the name was changed to GoldRoad.

Prospectors had been wandering the hills around Sitgeaves Pass since the 1850s and on occasion, they found small amounts of gold. In 1900, Jose Jerrez, a Mexican prospector in Mohave County was looking for his burro about 20 miles from Kingman when he stumbled upon a chunk of quartz that contained some gold. He packed up a few samples and contacted his friend, Henry Lovin of Kingman who quickly took the samples to an assayer. The quartz assayed at an amazing 40 ounces per ton! Jose had hit pay dirt.

Henry Lovin grubstaked Jose Jerrez in the amount of $16.00 and they wasted no time returning to the site to dig. Within a couple weeks, they dug a 15-foot shaft revealing more gold. Henry, realizing they couldn't dig all the gold out by themselves, found a buyer for the claim and sold it to a California group for $50,000. He gave his gold discovering partner, Jerrez, $26,000. Shortly after the sale, the California group sold their rights to another group of investors for $275,000. They brought in the necessary equipment to run a large operation, hired 180 miners and another Wild West gold rush was on. Soon hundreds of budding gold miners began swarming to the area looking for gold.

Henry invested his gold money wisely. Among other things, he opened a saloon called the Gold Road Club and the Gold Road Store in Acme Camp. He and his partner, J. S. Withers also developed several successful businesses including Lovin and Withers Mercantile in Kingman and a freight company and mercantile store in Oatman. Az. An advertisement in front of his liquor store read;

HENRY LOVIN -WHOLESALE DEALER IN ALL KINDS OF LIQUORS - WELCOME - NOT AFRAID OF TAINTED MONEY.

Henry Lovin came to Kingman in 1893 and was a true American success story. He grubstaked a prospector who discovered one of the largest gold strikes in Mohave County. Lovin operated a large ranch and a number of businesses. He was once a constable, twice-elected county sheriff, chosen to represent Mohave County in the Arizona Constitutional Convention, and was elected twice as the first state senator from the county. After that, he served as a county supervisor from 1925 until his death in 1931.

Ironically, Jose Jerrez, who was credited with the discovery of the gold, became one of Henry's best customers at the Goldroad Club Saloon. In true prospector fashion, Jerrez is said to have drunk and gambled away every nickel he made from the sale of the mine. Now broke and drunk, he went back to work as a laborer in the very mine he had discovered. Sadly, Jose Jerrez later ended his life by swallowing rat poison called ***Rough on Rats***.

(Rough on Rats was a poison used to kill vermin. It was composed of arsenic with a little coal added for coloring. Advertisements for its sale began appearing in the 1880's and soon became a household name. It was easily obtainable from chemists, but unfortunately, people started using it to take their own lives, especially those from the lower echelons of society.)

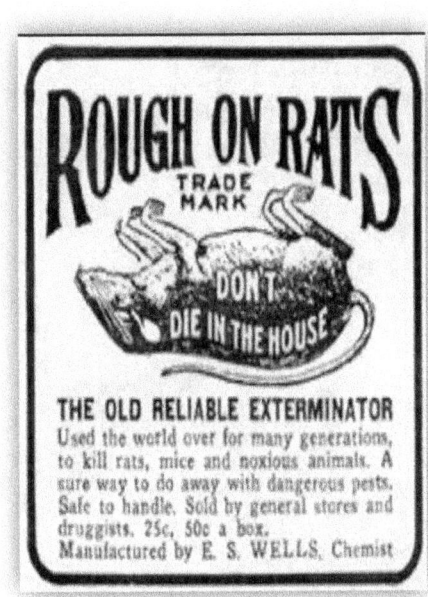

The package read,

"Don't let them die in the house. Rough on Rats clears out rats, mice, beetles, roaches, bed-bugs, ants, insects, moles, jackrabbits and gophers".

Here is how the August 8, 1908, edition of the Mohave County Miner newspaper reported the death of the famous gold discoverer, Jose Jerrez:

Yesterday Jose Jerrez, discoverer of the famous Gold Road mines, committed suicide at GoldRoad by taking 'Rough on Rats.' He lived several hours after taking the poison, suffering great pain. This single miner was buried in GoldRoad Cemetery. A stone monument was erected over his grave.

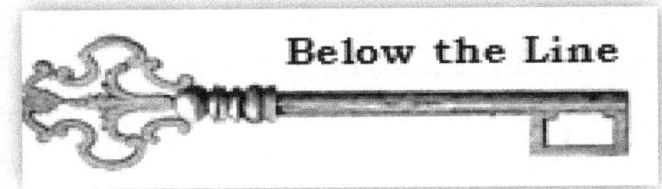

The lady with the white blouse is believed to be Jennie Bauters "Belgian Jennie". The tall man on the left is believed to be Clement C. Leigh "CC" Acme Az. Later known as GoldRoad c. 1903

The twenty-mile wagon trip to Acme Camp was over a rough and jarring trail that crossed a barren stretch of scorching desert. It was in no way a pleasant journey. The trip was hot, dusty and very slow going. When they arrived, Jennie was a little surprised at how isolated the Acme Camp was. Acme wasn't much more than a large campsite with tents and outhouses. But the good news was it was spilling over with men. In order for Jennie's business to succeed, there needed to be lots of men making plenty of money.

There was an old saying among brothel owners;
**"If the guys don't have money,
the gals don't get paid."**

The gold mining camp was nothing like the town of Jerome. After looking at the opportunities, of which there were few, Jennie settled on a crude building made of native stone with a rough timber roof. The building wasn't much, but Jennie knew that location was everything. The stone shack sat between two small businesses, "Carters" and the "Hog Ranch" and was just ten feet off the main road. The property also had a large flat backyard which would be perfect to set up tents for the working girls.

The stone shack in the front would become her saloon. Jennie would make do until she could build something better.

The plan was coming together, but Jennie had a lot of things to take care of before she could permanently pull up her stakes back in Jerome. She left C.C. in Acme Camp and returned to Jerome. She packed up her personal belongings and had them shipped by rail to Kingman, Arizona. Jennie then leased her bordello to a fellow competitor and promised some of her girls she would send for them once she got settled in Acme Camp. First, though, another journey was in Jennie's plans. She boarded a train to Chicago to visit her son Joseph, now a 21-year-old college student.

During her visit, she mentioned to her son, her plans to move to Acme Arizona, but was also cautious not to reveal exactly why. Joseph still did not know that the money for his education was coming from the spoils of her prostitution business. Joseph was her sole heir and would inherit her estate in the event of her death.

After a short visit with her son, Jennie headed back to Kingman to finalize her move to Acme Camp. Records show that she spent more than $550.00 on furniture and supplies at *the Lovin and Withers Mercantile in Kingman, Az. A newspaper ad featured the store's slogan "**WE WILL DELIVER THE GOODS EVEN IF IT BREAKS OUR BACKS.***

Jennie must have attracted quite a stir when her wagon came rolling into the dusty Acme Camp. Just the sight of a woman was quite unusual, much less a stagecoach stacked high with furniture, bed springs, supplies and several canvas tents.

Once everything was up and running, Jennie hung her new business sign above the front door. Her place was called "Below the Line" and with the help of Jennie and her girls, Acme soon became a wild and exciting place. The new frontier town, for now anyway, was void of any law enforcement and it was definitely a relief not to have anyone from the city breathing down her neck.

The prostitutes hung their undergarments on a clothesline as a form of advertising.

The red, lantern-lit path became deep and wide from all the foot traffic heading to the tents out the back of the saloon. Jennie wanted to be the first madam to mine this gold rush camp, but the mining she had planned was from the pockets of the miners themselves. Needless to say, business was booming.

There were card games, roulette, dice and you could bet on just about anything. Jennie also hired a honky-tonk piano player named Carlysle Wright to play late into the night on the weekends. Acme Camp turned out to be a personal gold mine for Jennie as the money rolled in from the reckless, thirsty miners. Bottles of whiskey stood like toy soldiers on the back bar. The price of whiskey was usually determined by how drunk she thought the customer was.

Unfortunately, as the story goes, less than two years after opening her doors, tragedy struck. A bartender named Lawson gave an account of what happened that dreadful September morning in 1905. He said, "Last night, Jennie was working in the saloon when Clement C. Leigh, all hopped up on opium stormed through the door and asked Jennie for money to pay a gambling debt. She refused. The next morning around eight o'clock, he came back into the saloon and started drinking. After a couple drinks, he left and went to find Jennie, who was still sleeping in her tent out back." Lawson continued, "About fifteen minutes later, around eight-thirty we heard a woman screaming, followed by several shots. I looked and saw Jennie Bauters running down the road barefoot. Her hair was down, she was still in her night clothes and Clement was in pursuit. He fired two shots and at least one hit Jennie in the hip. Then he fired a third shot. I saw Jennie fall in the dirt about thirty feet from her saloon. I heard Jennie pleading for her life. She was screaming something like, for God's sake, C. C., please, please don't shoot me! He responded by emptying his gun into Jennie. He shot her right in the face. I'll never get that picture out of my mind. It was terrible. Then a customer in the saloon ran to get the constable, Fred Brown."

In court, Lawson testified that even after Jennie was dead, Clement C. Leigh came back into the saloon, pointed his gun at him and demanded another shot of whiskey. Clement then reloaded his gun and walked out to Jennie's body lying there in the street. He shoved her head to the side with his boot and said, "Are you dead yet?" Lawson alleged that he then fired another shot that hit Jennie just behind her ear. Then I saw him point the pistol at his own chest and pull the trigger. He slowly laid down on the ground next to Jennie, put his hat over his face and crossed his feet.

Lawson said, "He just laid there, I guess figuring to die."

Another witness explained, "The pain on Jennie's once pretty, but now bloody and contorted face said it all as she made the sign of the cross and died right there in the dirt in front of her saloon. No one deserves to die like that."

Remarkably, Clement C. Leigh's suicide attempt failed. The bullet hit a rib and came to rest under his arm leaving nothing more than a slight gunshot wound and Leigh lived to pay dearly for his crime. The people of Acme were infuriated over Jennie's senseless killing and they wanted revenge.

At the time, Acme Camp had no law enforcement, so a group of citizens apprehended Clement C. Leigh and locked him in a makeshift holding cell until the Mohave County Sheriff could arrive. Jennie's bullet-ridden body was recovered from the road, leaving a large puddle of blood soaking into the dirt.

It was a stark reminder of just how callused this cold-blooded murder really was.

Back in Chicago, Jennie's son, Joseph was notified of the tragedy. He requested his mother's body be embalmed and held until his arrival. The problem was, the only morgue and embalming facility was 20 miles away by stagecoach in Kingman, Arizona.

The next day, the Mohave County Sheriff, Henry Lovin and Deputy John Harris arrived by stagecoach from Kingman. Clement C. Leigh, the accused murderer was handcuffed and placed in the stagecoach. The corpse of Jennie Bauters, now wrapped in a blood-soaked canvas rested on the bench seat across from Leigh in the coach. It had been more than 30 hours since her death and the effects of rigor mortis were setting in. Her corpse was bloated and the methane gases from her decaying body produced a horrible stench. Leigh, in pain from his wound, had plenty of time to reflect on his transgressions during the day-long ride back to Kingman. His punishment, however, had only just begun.

Upon arrival in Kingman, Leigh was locked up in the county jail and Jennie's body was taken to the morgue and held pending the arrival of her son. It took Joseph Phillipe Bauters five days by train to arrive from Chicago.

Joseph had been living in a modern, civilized city and had never been out West. He was extremely uneasy over how harsh and inhospitable the surroundings were. After all, Acme Camp was nothing but a camp of tents and crude, stone buildings in the hot, unforgiving desert. The real shock, however, was when Joseph learned that his now deceased mother had been nothing more than the madam of a camp-town whorehouse. Two passengers who rode the stagecoach to Goldroad with Jennie's son reported that the young man's anguish over losing his mother was the saddest case they had ever seen.

In the nine years that she lived in the United States, Jennie Bauters became the richest madam in the Arizona Territory. Obviously, in that time period she would have acquired a vast collection of personal possessions, but by the time her son arrived to claim her estate, most of her belongings had been ransacked. Thieves, drunks, drug addicts and even her fellow prostitutes swooped in like vultures on a carcass. Her fine clothes, fur coats, hats, shoes, jewelry, cash and all the liquor in her bar was cleaned out.

E. A. Shaw was the administrator of Jennie Bauters' estate. The probate court took an inventory of what remained of Jennie's estate and recorded the following;

This inventory provided a clear insight into the workings of Jennie's business and her profession.

1. $5,616.48 deposited in various banks. Several Un-cashed rent checks from both her house and her brothel on Main Street in Jerome, Arizona

2. Five lots in Jerome, Arizona

3. Acme Camp property and saloon inventory

4. Several lamps

5. Galvanized wash pans, pitchers and a bath tub.

6. A large painting of a nude woman above the bar.

7. A talking machine and twenty-eight records

8. Fancy pillows and lace bedding

9 Twelve night dresses

10. Three kimonos

11. Four tents with bed springs and mattresses

12. Misc. jewelry, a silver medallion, a lapel watch, a pair of gold plated cufflinks, shirt buttons, a silver hair brush set and, two French powder boxes.

```
Doz      ᵣisters Tooth Soap
         Sodium Hyposulphite
Doz      Seven Barks
Doz      Williams Shaving Sticks
Doz      Colgates Shaving Powder
         Cocoanut Oil
Doz      Drinking Tubes
         Gum Opium
Doz      Doans Kidney Pills
         ₘabs Morph 1/4 Gr   Lily
Doz      Taylors Oil Life
```

Also found among her personal effects were receipts for medicine, doctor bills and a locked, leather-bound book with names and client information.

Jennie's entire estate was worth a tidy sum. In fact, Joseph was about to inherit almost a half million dollars in today's currency. At the time though, he had no money of his own and had to take out a loan against his mother's estate to pay for her funeral.

Leigh's last shot had ripped through Jennie's head and it wasn't pretty. Her body was also decomposing rapidly making it impossible for a public viewing. Jennie needed to be laid to rest immediately. Joseph knew this and did his best to expedite his mother's burial. Joseph also felt that his mother, the richest woman in the Arizona Territory should be given a respectful burial in a proper cemetery in Kingman. These plans, however, were soon thwarted.

When the people of Kingman heard of Joseph's intent to bury his mother in the Pioneer Cemetery, many protested. They said there was no way they were going to allow some "dirty, low-life prostitute" to be buried next to their loved ones. The church believed that the sins that Jennie committed with her slayer had been that of an "unnatural and criminal pleasure and that her tragic fate was wholly deserved".

(Women of ill-repute were often ostracized by society. Many times throughout history, public cemeteries would not allow these women to be buried among their dearly departed. Sometimes authorities would agree to a burial outside the cemeteries perimeter or in a simple unmarked grave.)

Initially, Joseph Bauters was embarrassed and humiliated after learning about his mother's profession. After all, he had been raised by nuns in a Chicago convent under strict Christian beliefs. But soon, Joseph realized the hypocrisy of it all. The majority of the men in town had been drunk in his mother's saloon, gambled and even visited the women in the tents.

This injustice reminded him of a lesson taught to him by the nuns at St. Ignatius School: *John 8. "The scribes and the Pharisees* dragged the adulteress woman before Jesus with the intent of stoning her to death according to the Law of Moses". Jesus stood and said, "He that is without sin among you, let him cast the first stone". Convicted by their own sins, they walked away.

The spiteful behavior of the community seemed absurd, but in the end Joseph was forced to bury his mother just outside the Pioneer cemetery fence. Joseph was determined to rise above the fray and spared no expense when arranging the burial of his mother. Overall expenses included the cold storage at the morgue while waiting for Joseph to arrive from Chicago. The wagon delivery from Acme Camp to Kingman added $20.00. Caskets ranged in price from $7.50 for a pine box, to $117 for a high-end casket. He opted for a French draped casket with brass handles costing him $117.50.

Joseph hired gravediggers and even a carpenter to erect an elaborate monument surrounded by a white picket fence. Inside the coffin, Joseph placed his mother's leather journal of secrets along with the key and several items of jewelry.

Belgian Jennie was laid to rest on September 9, 1905. Jennie was widely known in Northern Arizona and not just because of the nature of her business. Records show her funeral was well attended by many of her close friends. Jennie Bauters was in no way void of human virtues. Her purse was always open to the needy and the manner she displayed was always within her proper latitude. Jennie possessed qualities and attributes that also attracted many acquaintances in typical society. She was recognized by many as being a very caring and charitable woman.

Jennie also supported an educated son who was the heir to her considerable estate. According to sources, her estate would have been notably larger had it not been for her unfortunate alliance with Leigh. It is said that he depended largely on her for financial support.

In general, though, Belgian Jennie was a savvy businesswoman. She owned two houses of prostitution and had a keen eye for real-estate. Jennie may have been the richest madam in the Arizona Territory, but she was best known as the "Madam with the heart of gold".

Grave of Jenny Bauter, Pioneer Cemetery, c.1907.
Courtesy Mohave Museum of History and Arts, Kingman.

Thieves Thick as Flies

After Jennie's burial, Joseph Bauters stayed in Arizona while his mother's estate was being settled. The predators, prostitutes and thieves were thick as flies in the Acme Camp.

Young Joseph, now 21 years of age was very vulnerable and certainly not akin to all the temptations this Wild West mining camp had to offer. I wasn't long before Joseph became obsessed with the working girls and began drinking and gambling away his new-found wealth.

After his mother's estate was settled, Joseph gathered up his new, real-world teachings and moved back to Chicago where he continued a lifestyle of self-destruction. Sadly, in his inebriated state, Joseph neglected to maintain his inheritance and lost all the property his mother had worked so hard to accumulate. With no one managing the properties in Jerome, Jennie's place was taken over by two Frenchmen who dallied in a practice known as "Demimonde".

*(**Demimonde" Demi-mond,** refers to a group of people who live self-indulgent lifestyles, usually in a flagrant and conspicuous manner. They are the affluent and pleasure-seeking portion of society unbound by morals, religion or tradition. Such behaviors often included drinking, drug use, gambling, high spending, fashion and sexual promiscuity, including homosexuality).*

Soon after taking over the building, both Frenchmen died violent deaths. The property was abandoned and left to ruin. Eventually, John Sullivan, the owner of the hotel next door, petitioned the courts to pay back-taxes and take over the abandoned building as part of his hotel. Unable to contact Joseph Bauters, the courts awarded the property to Sullivan.

Not much is known about the rest of Joseph Philippe Bauters's life. According to his descendants, the boy from Belgium that came to America and dreamed of a better life squandered away all his mother's wealth, and died an alcoholic on Chicago's "Skid Row" sometime in the 1930's.

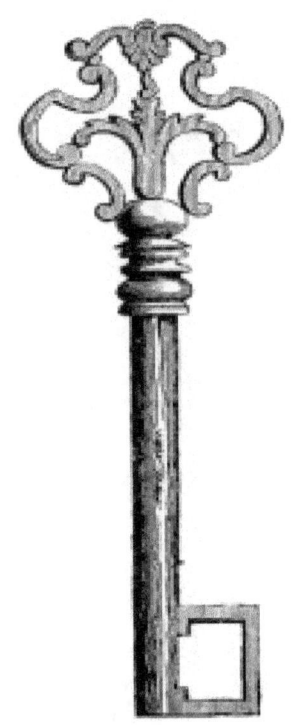

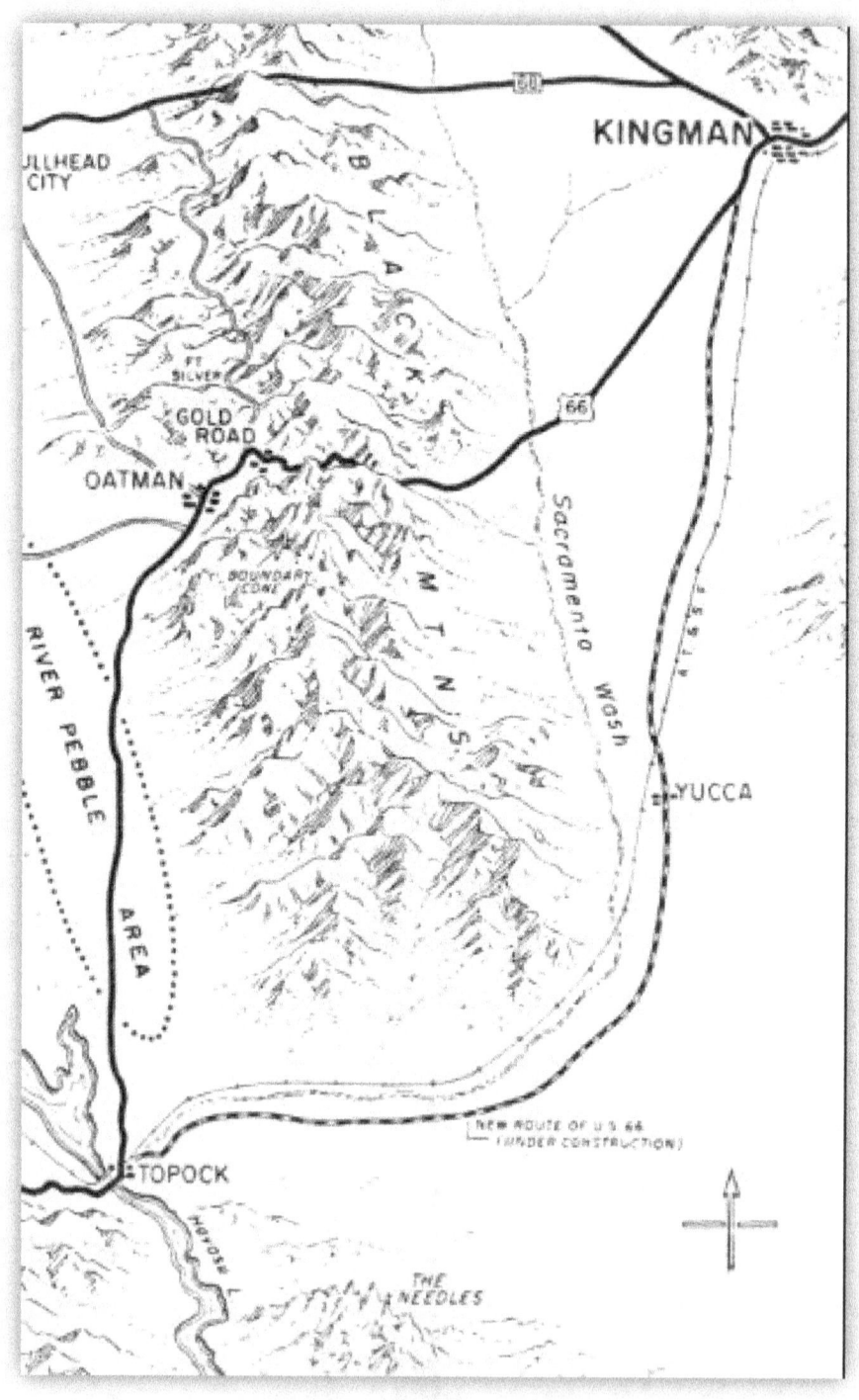

Moḥaue Co

January 18, 1907

More Dead Than Alive

Clement C. Leigh was found guilty of murder in the first degree, by a jury of twelve men for the murder of Jennie Bauters. Leigh wrote several letters and said farewell to his friends. He washed up, shaved and dressed in the suit of black clothes, white shirt, collar and tie all provided by the county. Leigh lurched forward against the cell bars cutting a deep gash on his forehead. Blood began pouring from the wound on his head. Two officers led him onto the scaffold and hurriedly prepared Leigh for the drop. More dead than alive presented a ghastly sight as the officers adjusted the noose around his neck, with blood trickling down his face landing on his white shirt.

Clement C. Leigh sat in jail for 18 months as he awaited trial for the murder of Jennie Bauters. Leigh had always assumed a seemingly untroubled attitude toward the whole situation and in fact, told various stories of what happened concerning Jennie's murder.

In one account, he claimed he was passing Jennie's tent when she called to him to give her a cigarette. He entered the tent and soon began quarreling about another man with whom Jennie desired to live with in preference to him. Clement said Jennie called him a vile name and started to run away while screaming she was going after a gun. He recalled being wildly angered and shooting her, but couldn't remember how many times. He then concluded by explaining why he shot himself. Clement said he knew the legal trouble that was awaiting him, and then after she was dead, he saw no sense in living anymore.

Leigh was eventually found guilty by a jury of twelve men for the first-degree murder of Jennie Bauters and the death penalty was ordered. Leigh's mother, assisted by Attorney Leroy Anderson of Yavapai County used every means possible to secure a reprieve of her son's death sentence. A letter was sent to Governor Kibbey, but after careful review of the evidence, he refused to interfere. They even sent a telegram to President Roosevelt asking for a stay of execution, but never received a response.

Leigh was notified of his sentence in the early morning of January 18, 1907 and immediately began preparing for the end. He wrote several letters and said goodbye to a few friends. He washed up, shaved and dressed in a white shirt and black suit provided by the county. When the sheriff and two officers appeared at the cell door, Leigh asked if they had come for him. The sheriff answered yes and read the death warrant out-loud. Just as he finished reading, Leigh gave out a yell and charged forward, smashing his head against the cell bars. A deep gash on his forehead resulted and blood began pouring from the wound.

The two officers led the bleeding, semi-conscious Leigh outside and headed straight up the hangman's gallows. As the hangman placed the noose around his neck, Leigh's eyes opened slightly and almost seemed oblivious as to what was happening. With blood streaming down his face onto his clean white shirt, Clement Leigh already seemed more dead than alive and presented quite a ghastly sight.

"The trap-door sprung at precisely 2:00 pm on January 18, 1907, and Clement Leigh plunged to his death. Once there was no discernible movement, the body was allowed to hang for thirty more minutes before a doctor pronounced him dead and the body was cut down.

It is believed that Leigh's neck was snapped and became detached from his spine in the drop. His head hung limp. They placed Clement Leigh's body in a coffin and buried him inside the Pioneer Cemetery in Kingman, Arizona, all at the county's expense. To some, this all seemed quite ironic since his victim Jennie Bauters was forced to be buried outside the boundaries of the same cemetery.

Talk about School Spirits

Without anyone to care for Jennie's gravesite, the elaborate memorial that Joseph had erected began to decay in the harsh desert climate. The white picket fence surrounding her grave rotted and fell to ruins and the headstone and wooden cross became unreadable. Before long, Mother Nature had completely reclaimed the site, leaving little evidence of its very existence.

Over the years, many cemeteries in Arizona have been moved or destroyed for highways, commercial enterprises, parks, public schools and public works. In 1917 Mohave County donated the Pioneer Cemetery property to the school district for a new high school. Construction was to commence, pending the removal and reburial of all gravesites. The notice was given and it was up to the surviving families to make the necessary arrangements.

Today, part of Lee Williams High School sits atop the former Pioneer Cemetery. Everything within its boundaries was eventually leveled and headstones that could not be clearly read were bulldozed into a nearby wash.

The Pioneer Cemetery in Kingman existed from 1900 thru 1917. It was the final resting place for at least 400 souls. Early settlers, miners, railroad workers and more than 70 Native American tribal members called Hualapai (People of the tall pines) were buried at the Pioneer Cemetery. Prior to 1909, death certificates on the roster did not show the exact plot, but simply listed the Pioneer Cemetery as the burial place.

After the Mountain View cemetery opened in 1914, officials began moving bodies out of Pioneer Cemetery and over to the Mountain View Cemetery. The fee imposed for the move was $45.00, *($600 in today's currency)*. But the charge per body proved to be too high a price in war-time America and as a result, some of the departed were not moved. If families couldn't afford the fee, or no one came forward to claim them, the graves remained where they were. The cemetery was formally abandoned in 1944. In 1948, Kingman Junior High was built next to the old cemetery site. Kingman High School was built on an adjacent site in 1957 and then took over the junior high buildings in 1972.

Occasionally, youngsters began to notice bones surfacing as they played on the new football field. Many organizations were alarmed and some took action to have the existing remains collected and placed in a solitary grave. A plaque dedicated to the unidentified pioneers was then placed on the site. It was a disturbing and unfortunate incident, but most felt that it had been dealt with appropriately and that the issue was resolved.

The plaque read;

(We humbly dedicate this ground, the site of Kingman's first cemetery in memory of the founding pioneers who were interred in these hallowed grounds. 1861-1920, Erected May 20, 1963.")

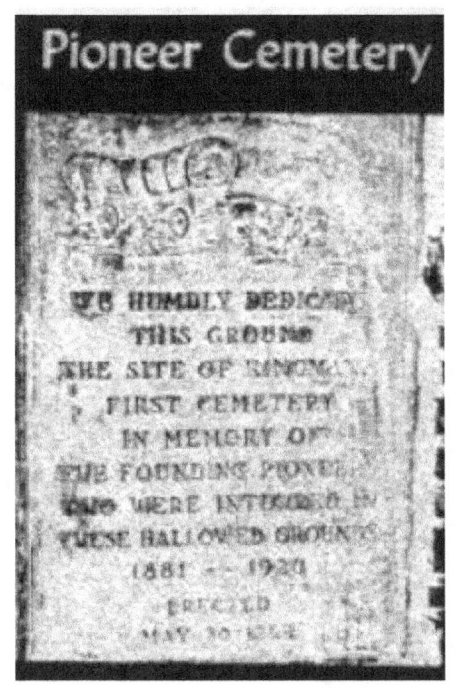

This location can be a little confusing for some, as this campus has been changed several times to accommodate different schools and grades during the last decade and a half.

Over the years, students claim they've seen apparitions of men and women in 19th Century clothing lurking in the hallways. Some report they've heard the sound of Native American drums beating. There are also many reports of disembodied footsteps, flickering lights, alarms, hand dryers and motion detectors that go off for no reason. Spectators, during graduation events and football games have witnessed a female ghost in a nightgown and a man in a bowler hat on the football field. Many students, staff and residents are convinced that the high school is indeed haunted by the ghosts of the early pioneers and the Hualapai Indians who were buried beneath these school grounds.

This story, however, was far from over as the eeriness of it all rose to a new level. The Kingman Daily Miner reported the following on July 30, 2010.

DAILYMINER

7/30/2010

**The Daily Miner of Kingman reported
7/ 30/ 2010:**

Workers with CORE Construction were digging a trench behind the bleachers for a sewer line Tuesday on what used to be the southern end zone of the Lee Williams High School football field. They began unearthing bone fragments. "In any old town like ours, especially one that involved mining, railroad, cattle and Indian battles things don't always go so well," said Diane Silverman, a supervisor at the Kingman tourism office. "People die for all kinds of reasons. And they didn't all go away happy." Many were buried in the old Pioneer Cemetery. Fifty workers digging a trench behind the bleachers shockingly unearthed eleven turn-of-the-century graves. Several of the graves did not contain coffins and the bodies appeared to have been wrapped in Indian blankets. It is believed that these were most likely deceased members of the "Hualapai Indian Tribe".

In addition to the Human remains unearthed there were pieces of wood and what looked like to be brass handles and a name plate from a high-end coffin. Other artifacts included cuff links, a silver medallion and several pieces of jewelry.

To say the least, the workers became every uneasy digging in the old graveyard. Because of the disturbance of the Native Hualapai graves, the current Hualapai tribal elder, Drake Havatone was called in.

The tribal elder, Havatone said, "We believe it is forbidden to move or disturb a body because the spirits become restless. Sometimes the ghost-spirits even become angry." Havatone performed a ceremony to pacify the spirits. He blessed all the spirits, along with the workers who had disturbed the graves".

Havatone added, "Spirits of the dead will sometimes follow the person that disturbed them, home. He hoped that the cleansing of the workers had pacified the troubled spirits".

CORE Construction Co. Superintendent Roger Jacks said, "The discovery of the remains has caused slight delays in construction. Our larger concern is over the remains and the proper handling of them. Workers have about another 100 feet of excavating work. It's a sensitive situation, but it's being handled in the proper manner. The medical examiner's office and officials from the CORE Construction Co. are working together in the effort." Should any more remains be found, their location will be marked with a GPS unit, removed by the medical examiner and stored at their Lake Havasu facility until a final resting place is determined.

Hualapai Indian Mothers with children
displaying their beautiful hand-woven
blankets. Circa, early 1900's

More Ghost Theories

Jennie rested peacefully just outside the old Pioneer Cemetery's boundaries for more than a century. Because of the location and the objects unearthed matching those buried with Jennie, some people believe that this gravesite was indeed Belgian Jennie's

Then, in an instant, she was violently ripped from her grave by a diesel powered, earth moving monster and her bones scattered about. To add insult to injury, some of Jennie's remains were thrown into a five gallon Home Depot bucket and stored in a Lake Havasu maintenance yard facility.

As mentioned earlier, while a spirit may have initially passed on, it will often return if their grave is vandalized, tombstone stolen or other desecrations of the grave occurs.

Some believe that this cruel disrespect left Belgian Jennie's spirit tormented and confused. In the past several years there have been numerous reports of a woman dressed in her night clothes, carrying a skull down the darkened streets of GoldRoad, Oatman, Kingman, and Jerome. Some have attempted to follow this mysterious woman, but she simply disappears into the darkness.

Bear in mind, Clement C. Leigh was hung for his crime, and in the drop, they claim that his skull became detached from his neck. In 1944, Leigh's remains were exhumed with the others from the Lee Williams High School grounds. His remains were placed in the same solitary grave as the others. There was, however, one important piece missing. During the excavation of the property, his skull was apparently left behind and plowed into a nearby wash.

There has been a great deal of evidence collected over the past decade or so. The majority of it comes from "paranormal investigators". Many believe that earth-bound spirits simply do not know they are dead. These "ghost hunters" spend time at alleged haunted sites with an array of equipment, hoping to communicate with the spirit world.

For example, on January 22, 2015, Zack Bagans and the team from *"Ghost Adventures"* filmed a television episode at the old Lee Williams High School.

Today Lee Williams High School in Kingman, Arizona, is listed among the *"Ten Most Haunted Schools in America"*. It is situated on the grounds of the old Pioneer Cemetery and some claim it is haunted by restless phantoms from a previous century.

Since the beginning of recorded history, thousands of ghostly experiences have been documented by people from around the world. Of course there is no concrete proof that ghosts really exist, however, there are many theories to explain their possible existence. Some assert that a "departed one" might remain in our world for one of the following reasons;

1. One theory is that a ghost is a human spirit that has passed out of the physical body, but for some reason is stuck between this plane of existence and the next. This could be a result of some tragedy or distress.

2. A sudden death leaves them confused, they have unfinished business or they struggle with an intense fear of judgment.

3. One interesting theory, (one that might be hard to wrap your head around) claims that past events somehow have recorded themselves. What we see as a ghost is really just history playing back. There is no spirit present at all. It's sort of like watching a movie.

4. A less popular explanation, for obvious reasons, is that ghosts are just the subconscious mind at work and they are only a figment of your imagination. This might suggest that maybe the ghosts you are seeing aren't real and perhaps you have psychological issues at hand, which are causing you to hallucinate.

5. Some physicists theorize there may be many different dimensions and timelines as well as ours.

6. Then there are people who just prefer to dismiss the idea altogether and simply say there is no such thing as ghosts.

After reviewing the facts I've laid out in this book, you can decide for yourself if you think ghosts do or do not exist. Regardless, the fact remains that until science can come up with some definitive answers, no one knows for sure if ghosts are real.

One thing we do know, however, is that Belgian Jennie was a kind soul and was never known to hold contempt for anyone. Many have said, "Belgian Jennie had a heart of gold.

JENNIE WAS A KIND SOUL

Belgian Jennie had a hart of gold.
Shot down in cold blood we're told.
Her silent screams cry out,
as her unseen shadow moves about.
She haunts the desert looking for her lover
His severed skull she has discovered.
Her silent screams cry out,
as her unseen shadow moves about.
Her ghost on this earth will forever roam,
Pleading unmercifully to just go home
Her silent screams cry out,
as her unseen shadow moves about
by Peggy Hicks

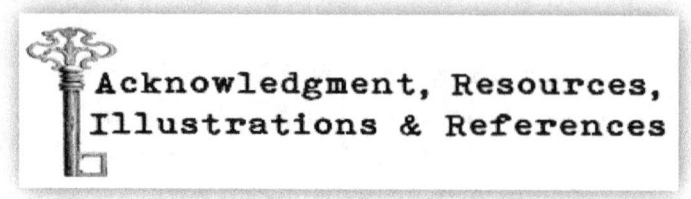

Acknowledgment, Resources, Illustrations & References

ACKNOWLEDGMENTS

Jerome Historical Society Archives

Melanie Sturgeon -The Journal of Arizona History

Nancy Smith-Historian-Women of the Half World

History of Four Years 1896-1900 by C.A. Brown

RESOURCES & REFERENCES

Library of Congress Ellis Island Immigration
1880-1920's Records

Arizona Pioneer & Cemetery Research

Mohave County Court House Records

Mohave County Historical Society

Jerome Historical Society Archives

Hartcort Press, 1946.
"Jerome - The Wickedest City" by William Wingfield

ARIZONA NEWSPAPER ACCOUNTS

Daily Miner, Kingman Arizona, July 30, 2010.

Coconino Sun, November 25, 1905, Page 2

Arizona Republican, January 06, 1906, Page 2

Arizona Republican, January 17, 1907, Page 10

Mohave County Miner - January 19, 1907

Bisbee Daily Review, Monday, January 20, 1907

ILLUSTRATIONS

Ellis Island Foundation Inc,
Button hook men, Luggage, and health

Jerome Historical Society Plaque Project

Find a grave- Jennie Bauters grave in 1907

Mohave County Vital Records
Certificate of Death- for Clement C. Leigh

Private Collection - Vintage Post Cards and Photos

Clement C. Leigh
Certificate of Death
By Hanging Circa 1907

CERTIFICATE OF DEATH.

A. E. EALY, Heath Officer,

KINGMAN, MOHAVE COUNTY, ARIZONA.

No body can be legally interred until a permit has been issued until there shall have been delivered to the proper official a certificate of Death made in the manner directed. See back of form for directions. WRITE PLAINLY WITH EXPANSIVE INK. THIS IS A PERMANENT RECORD.

Full name of Deceased _____ C. C. Leigh

PERSONAL AND STATISTICAL PARTICULARS AND MEDICAL CERTIFICATE OF DEATH

Sex ___ M ___ Color ___ White ___ Age ___ 35 ___ Years _____ Months _____ Days

Place of Birth ___ Illinois ___ Lived in Arizona _____ yr _____ Years.
(State or Country)

Occupation ___ Miner _____

Died on the _____ day of _____ 1907, about ___ 2 ___ A. M.

Place of Death ___ Kingman ___ *Single, Married, Widower or Divorce

Place of Burial ___ Kingman _____
(Township, Village or City, If in City, number of street and Ward)

Name of Undertaker ___ Don Morris _____ Date of Burial _____
(Cemetery)   Address ___ Kingman A.T.

CAUSE OF DEATH.

	DURATION			
	Years	Months	Days	Hours
Immediate Cause ___ Hanging	—	—	—	—
Contributory Cause or Complication	—	—	—	—

I HEREBY CERTIFY, that the above stated personal particulars are true to the best of my knowledge and belief, and that the cause of death of the above named and described deceased was as above written by me, and my name is registered with the Health Office.

WITNESS MY HAND, This _____ day of _____ 190 ___

(Signature) ___ Dr. M. G. Davis _____
(Physician, Midwife or Coroner.)

Address ___ Kingman _____

*Erase as facts require.

Jennie Bauters Aka "Belgian Jennie Acme Camp, (Goldroad) Arizona 1904

Model T's At Kingman's Pioneer Cemetery in 1913. These Graves Were Moved To The Mountain View Cemetery The Following Year.

Hualapai (Walapai) Indian Couple
Kingman, Arizona, Circa 1902

Front Door of "Belgian Jennie's" House in Jerome, Arizona before the House Was Torn Down

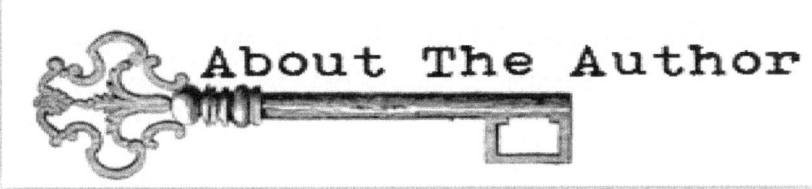

About The Author

Peggy Hicks was born at home in rural Colorado in 1953. Being the oldest of ten siblings, she soon began telling imaginary tales to keep her little brothers and sisters amused. At the early age of 12 years old, she published a short play that was purchased by the well-known educational publisher, Scott Foresman. Growing up in the sixties, with guitar in hand, she began turning her stories into poems and her poems into folk songs which she sometimes performed at local gatherings and auditoriums. She has since added many credits to her name as a musician, writer, narrator, real estate agent and local historian. She is active in her local community and chamber of commerce. Peggy is the proud mother of five grown children, three boys and two girls, with a total of ten grandchildren. Today, Peggy lives with her longtime partner Dennis in the beautiful foothills of Mingus Mountain just outside of Jerome. The two of them own and operate a rock and gift shop in Jerome called "Arizona Discoveries".

They love to inform and entertain the tourists who drop by their gift shop

Author Peggy Hicks combines her interest in Madams of the Wild West, common ghost theories along with her passion for Arizona history into one of kind of stories. She is also the author of two other books, both available on Kindle and Amazon.

1. The Ghost of the Cuban Queen Bordello, the story of a 1920's Jerome Arizona Madam

2. Ghost Town Stories and Wicked Legends of Jerome, Arizona.

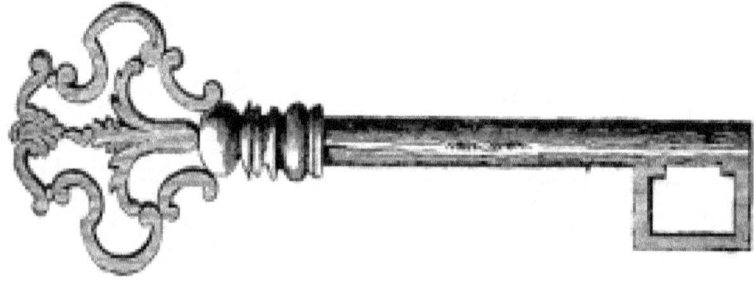